A MAN TO TRUST

Alexa Lockton has a thriving car business and her fiancé, Royston Wentworth, is an eminently suitable future husband. But when she employs Rick Markland to work in her garage, her ordered world crumbles. Against Royston's cautious prudence, Rick encourages bold expansion at Lockton's. Alexa is caught between the two men — for she finds that Rick is compellingly attractive and, as she plans her forthcoming marriage, she begins to wonder how long she can resist his magnetic appeal.

Books by Angela Dracup
in the Linford Romance Library:

AN INDEPENDENT SPIRIT
A TENDER AMBITION

ANGELA DRACUP

A MAN TO TRUST

Complete and Unabridged

LINFORD
Leicester

First published in Great Britain in 1987 by
Robert Hale Limited
London

First Linford Edition
published 2006
by arrangement with
Robert Hale Limited
London

British Library CIP Data

Dracup, Angela
A man to trust.—Large print ed.—
Linford romance library
1. Love stories
2. Large type books
I. Title
823.9′14 [F]

ISBN 1–84617–182–2

Published by
F. A. Thorpe (Publishing)
Anstey, Leicestershire

Set by Words & Graphics Ltd.
Anstey, Leicestershire
Printed and bound in Great Britain by
T. J. International Ltd., Padstow, Cornwall

This book is printed on acid-free paper

1

'Not join the business!' Bess Markland straightened from the serious task of pouring two glasses of her best vintage claret and looked in amazement at her grandson. 'But why — for heavens sake — why?'

Rick Markland winced internally but faced his grandmother without flinching. Dressed in a wide-shouldered grey cashmere trouser suit, with a flashing grape-sized diamond brooch on the lapel, she was just sufficiently off-centre of good taste to be sensational. Not bad for seventy, he thought. She was the one person in the world he would wish to avoid hurting if there was any way round it. But there was no way round it. It had taken weeks of tough self-debate to reach his decision but he believed that he had made the right one. He owed it to Bess to share his thoughts — openly and with complete honesty. To do any less would be to make a mockery of their good relationship.

She walked across to him, her tall frame slim and erect. 'There,' she said severely, placing a chunky cut-glass goblet on the dainty mahogany table beside him. 'I hope that gives you the strength to explain your amazing statement — and me the strength to listen and understand! Cheers!'

Rick twirled the glass slowly so that it gathered all the fragments of the late afternoon sunshine into its depths and shot them forth as flashing fiery needles. He looked at the label on the bottle standing on the marble mantelpiece and whistled softly. 'Château Latour 1973 — that's going it a bit even for you, Bess!' He had long since dropped the term grandmother for which she had always shown considerable distaste.

'Yes,' she eyed him with shrewd appraisal, 'this was going to be a celebration — having you back from six months in France, the advent of your finally taking over the reins at Markland's — and the anticipation of my having a little rest at long last. Remember?' she admonished.

Guilt seared him like a hot rapier but he knew Bess was strong. He was certain she could cope with what he had to propose. He stared into the fireplace where a pile of logs burned in the dog-grate in a whispering sigh of pink and yellow flames. Once again he rotated the goblet then sniffed at the wine appreciatively with the acute assessment of the connoisseur. 'You know,' he said tentatively, 'my tutor at Oxford maintained that a taste for excellent claret in anyone under thirty is a sign of an over-indulged youth.'

Bess glanced at him sharply. His usual light bantering tone seemed to be completely missing today. 'Are you accusing me of over-indulging you, Rick?' She made a swift, anxious mental review of those childhood years when he had been entirely her responsibility. 'Surely you wouldn't tar me with the brush of a silly doting old granny?'

His characteristic grin broke out over the strong, clearly defined features. 'No — I certainly wouldn't!'

'What then?' She asked with acidic bite. 'What are you trying to tell me?'

Rick tried to find the right words to introduce her gently to what was on his mind. They eluded him. A silence grew between them, taking its grip on the big drawing-room like an injection of anaesthetic. 'I've been one of the lucky ones, Bess,' he said at last.

She pursed her lips. 'I'm not sure that being fatherless at six, having one's mother depart to California a year later with a wealthy wine-grower and being brought up by a succession of nannies and a working grandmother was all that lucky! Hardly a bed of roses!'

He looked thoughtful. 'I had security, good friends, lots of fun, a wonderful place to live . . . and I had you,' he finished challengingly.

A dark flush of warmth crept up her cheeks.

'You let me be the person I wanted to be. You didn't make me fit into a pre-shaped mould — and I had plenty of friends whose parents made them do just that. Some of them are pretty screwed up now!' he finished quietly.

'Ah well,' she smiled, 'I was parenting second time round. I suppose I'd learned a few lessons.'

Rick leaned forward, his voice low with urgency. 'I loved it at Oxford,' he said, 'I loved reading Shakespeare and Donne, sipping wine with my tutor, drinking beer with the guys and flirting with those gorgeous brainy girls. But when I went to the Business School in London I saw another slice of life. I met men and women who've never had the chances I had — great people with lively minds and bags of drive. Some of them had done all sorts of jobs to supplement their grants and send money home to their families.' He paused and gave her one of his direct, raking gazes. 'I felt rather humble, felt I'd had things too easy.'

She arched her eyebrows. 'Idealistic youth!' she murmured to herself.

His sharp ears caught the comment. 'I've reached my mid-twenties, Bess. I'm past being a youngster. Time I took on some real responsibility.'

'Yes! Join the business!' she told him vehemently.

His brilliant blue eyes blazed with determination. 'I'm not ready to join the business,' he asserted strongly, then added softly, 'not yet.'

She closed her eyes as though a great weight had descended on her. 'How long have you been thinking this? Why didn't you tell me?'

'I didn't tell you because I didn't want to hurt you needlessly. I had to be absolutely sure. I've been unhappy about the plans for me to come into the business and take a seat on the board for some time now.'

'But why?' she asked in complete bewilderment.

'Because I'm not qualified,' he said flatly.

'Not qualified! You have a first-class Oxbridge Degree, six months experience with a firm in France and a Diploma in Business Management!' She gave a somewhat unladylike snort.

'But I have no experience of the real world of work, no knowledge of life beyond the walls of a superb school, the best university in the world and an internationally renowned business school.'

'Oh dear!' Bess stared at his amiable features knowing that beneath the relaxed, laconic exterior was a will of iron. His strength of purpose had always matched her own and probably now exceeded it as he had come to full maturity and she was no longer in her vigorous prime.

He regarded her steadily across the fresh chasm of silence.

'Well,' she sighed, 'I can see that you've made up your mind. I know better than to attempt to persuade you otherwise. You know, Rick — when you were a little boy I thought you were so filled with life and energy that you would take the world by storm. Don't throw all that away — will you? Don't waste it all — whatever it is you plan to do!'

He looked into her eyes, saw the sadness of the years in their depths, noted the deep trenches that the determination for survival had carved into her skin. 'When I was a boy,' he said gravely, 'I thought you were the most wonderful, powerful woman in the world!'

'How perceptive of you!' she said drily.

'And,' he added, 'I have no intention of throwing away any of my advantages — my life and energy as you call them.'

'Well that's a relief,' she said in acerbic tones. 'So what is it that you *do* intend to do? Let's get down to the nitty-gritty. The suspense is terrible.'

'That's exactly it, Bess,' he said with wry humour, 'that's what I want to get down to — the nitty-gritty. I want to experience the grittiness of life, the grittiness of work — boring, routine, humdrum work!'

Bess was thunderstruck. She had never had an inkling that he cherished any desire to deviate from the smooth path which would take him from higher education into a position of top management in the family business — *her* business since her husband died twelve years ago. But then Rick had always held strong ideas of his own and when he truly believed in something he was totally immovable. His judgement had usually been remarkably good. She was prepared to give him a serious hearing.

His blue eyes pierced hers with the glitter of intent. 'Bess — give me your blessing to have one year — just one year to test myself out in the world without the security of your money.'

Bess considered the statement seriously and at length. 'Do you know — this is the very first time I can remember you asking me for something I was reluctant to agree to.'

'I never had to ask. You always knew, always understood.'

'You were never greedy,' she responded drily.

'I was always damned lucky!'

She got up and walked across to the window. Outside the grass shivered under the thinning clouds and a watery sun glided its silver fingers across the bare limbs of the great monkey puzzle tree which presided over the curved driveway. Spring in the north of Yorkshire was rarely a gentle season. 'So what is it you want to do?' she asked in quiet resignation.

'Get a job. A plain, ordinary job and work damned hard. It won't be wasted time, Bess. When I take my seat on the board I'll be one hell of a better manager. I'll have more sympathy — more insight for the people working with me.'

You seem to have rather more insight than most already, she thought privately. She felt rather proud of him.

One or two of her friends' sons and grandsons had been quite content to drift along in comfortable jobs, their luxurious life-styles drawn from the proceeds of the hard work of previous generations. She considered her own youth, the hard grind as a machinist in a factory manufacturing raincoats where she met and fell in love with James Markland, a young accountant with visions of starting a business on his own. Rick, of course, had never known what that kind of hardship was. She hoped he never did. The irony of his plan struck her sharply. 'So,' she remarked wryly, 'you'll travel the world and bring back the Holy Grail. Where will you get a job?'

'I don't know yet — but I'll get one. I don't intend to go far afield. I'll be around if you need me.'

'You're good,' she said simply. 'Kind as well — ' she murmured as though he were not there. She recalled his amazing gentleness as a growing giant of a teenager when he would rescue cats stranded up the great trees in the garden and once had spent hours carefully removing bricks from the back of the chimney-breast in order to free a frantic trapped starling.

'Bess?' he said enquiringly.

'Sorry, I'd gone off into my fuddled old head. It's the shock you've given me!' she joked.

'There's nothing fuddled about your head!' he grinned.

She switched herself firmly back into the present. 'It might not be easy to get a job, Rick. Non-skilled work is at a premium like everything else — you're ridiculously over-qualified.'

'Yes — I think I'll have to keep that rather quiet.' He smiled at her conspiratorially. 'Bess, you've taken this so well. I'm really grateful.' He ran a hand through his thick hair — a gesture which was so familiar to her, indicating that his easy-going composure had been temporarily disturbed.

'I'm not bowled over with delight,'

she said severely, 'Don't run away with that idea.'

He moved across to her and seized her hands impulsively.

'I'll be O.K. Really. You mustn't worry about me!'

'I won't,' she said a little grimly, 'you're tough — a survivor. You'll not come to any harm.'

He felt the hands tremble under his and his heart shifted with feeling. He looked down at her fingers, swollen and veined now with age. 'Hey,' he said softly, noticing the big ruby on the little finger of her left hand, 'that's beautiful. Mother used to wear it, didn't she? I remember as a kid it would flash in the dark when she came to say goodnight to me.' He stared with interest at the stone — rosy as a Caribbean sunset and as fat as a Brazil nut.

Bess spread out her fingers recalling that they had once been as white and smooth as eggshells and regretted the ugliness the years had laid on them. 'The Markland ring,' she smiled, 'I gave it to your mother when she and your father got engaged. She sent it back to me just recently — said she felt she no longer had a right to it. I rather think she has a few new and sizable gems from husband number two. Anyway it's too small now for my knobbly old knuckles.' She glanced up at him. 'You've only to find a lovely slender-fingered young woman to settle down with and I'll hand it over with pleasure,' she joked lightly.

Rick raised an amused eyebrow. 'Mmn,' he said with mocking severity, 'I've other things than marriage on my mind at present. Plenty of time for that later!' He grinned with the wickedness of a good-natured, free-wheeling bachelor.

'Ah well — I suppose so.' She eyed him sadly. 'I suppose it's all settled then. I'm going to have to resign myself to doing without you at Marklands for a while longer.'

He saw her eyes prick with moisture and his filled with compassion. He enveloped her in a great bear-like hug. 'I'll keep in touch, I'll be around for anything you need. Promise!'

She walked down the steps with him wrapping her grey calf-length fox fur around her tightly against the fierce chill. Rick was adjusting his black crash helmet, zipping up the thick padded jacket.

Bess eyed his current form of transport — a gleaming BMW 1,000-c.c. cycle — as though it were some gargantuan malevolent insect from a science fiction film. 'That infernal machine,' she complained, 'why can't you get yourself a nice sensible car, then you could wear a nice sensible suit — perhaps even a tie!'

Rick roared with affectionate laughter. 'All in good time — all in good time,' he told her placatingly.

'Let me know where you're staying as soon as you get a place,' she commanded, grimacing as the machine exploded into a frenzy of unremitting roaring.

She watched as he gathered speed down the drive, making the daffodils which poked up through the grass quiver in alarm. When the waning note of the engine was no more than an echo in her head she walked slowly back up the steps already wondering which haulage firm would be the best to undertake the delicate task of transporting two cases of her best claret to some dreary downtown lodgings. She could still indulge him a little if she liked. She'd got to that age when one can do quite a lot of what one likes without worrying unduly.

* * *

A slender hand, its skin as creamy as a peeled banana, reached over the desk and rested on the handset of the slimline push button phone. 'Don't ring!' its owner instructed, 'not just for a minute or two.' She raised her head to look at her secretary who stood in front of the desk, a pencil tucked behind her car, a sheaf of papers in her arms and a broad grin on her face.

'The day that phone stops ringing we'll all be out on the streets singing for a crust,' she chuckled, eyeing her boss appreciatively.

Alexa nodded briefly. 'True — but I need to sort out this morning with you first. I'm not quite sure how we'll pack everything in.'

'We will; we always do. *You* always do at any rate.'

Alexa Lockton's secretary, appropriately named Hope, placed her plump, cuddlesome body into one of Alexa's squashy crinkled leather chairs and awaited instructions.

Alexa tapped a pearly coral nail against her ivory white front teeth — a sure sign that she was concentrating on a number of problems.

'Did anybody ever tell you,' Hope said thoughtfully, 'that your hair is the colour of a polished conker. It's a perfect knock-out. Nature is really quite unfair to give some people such wonderful advantages.'

'I can't recall its being mentioned,' Alexa smiled, half impatient, half touched. 'You're an incurable romantic,' she added drily, wanting to press on with business matters and already deep into her diary. 'Mmn,' she murmured, 'Morris is expecting me at eleven, I need to check that the work has been done on that M.G. Maestro, there's the invoice to prepare for the Rover going out tomorrow.'

She paused, frowning slightly. 'And then there's the advert to do for Saturday's paper. Heavens! Does the newspaper have a deadline around noon?'

'Yes.' Hope was scribbling away on her pad. 'I'll take care of the ad. We can draft it out before you go.'

'I've overbooked myself,' Alexa frowned. 'How stupid. And I'm cooking dinner for Royston tonight as well!'

'Don't worry, you'll be fine. You could cancel Royston of course!' Hope suggested wickedly.

'Hope!' Alexa warned.

'Sorry, I must show more respect. He is your one and only betrothed after all!'

A spark of discomfort shot through Alexa's chest. It worried her that Hope — this assistant on whom she depended so much, who was such a good friend, should so openly question the desirability of her future husband.

Hope peered down into the street where a big blond man was polishing a sleek gold Rover. 'There he is,' she chuckled, 'Super-man; hard at it. It was certainly your lucky day when *he* turned up.'

'Mmn,' Alexa's gaze followed Hope's. 'I must say he pulls his weight, he's an excellent worker.'

'And what a hunk!' Hope added. 'Six foot two and eyes of blue.'

Alexa clicked her tongue in amused exasperation. Rick Markland had more than earned his keep as car cleaner, driver and general dogsbody since she had taken him on two months previously. The fact that he was powerfully and intensely male she had deliberately chosen to ignore.

Not so Hope, however. 'He really is beautiful,' she concluded in open admiration.

Alexa threw a glance heavenward. She was well aware of Hope's taste in men; rakish, macho, on the scruffy side, and loaded up with sex appeal — all of which applied to Rick. He had the warm open smile of a man used to making an impact on women.

He was, nevertheless, endlessly flexible, unflaggingly energetic and remarkably quick at grasping the nature of her business.

She would be very hard-pressed to do without him at the moment.

'I must rush,' she muttered. 'Morris hates unpunctuality.'

'*You* hate unpunctuality,' Hope corrected her, smiling. 'And there's no need to rush back. We'll hold the fort beautifully — me and Rick.' She arched her eyebrows coyly.

'You're a diamond,' Alexa informed

her affectionately.

And you're a peach, Hope thought, sneaking an admiring glance at her boss, taking note of the alert hazel eyes, the straight small nose, the coral-tinted mouth that was resolute yet softly sensual. The delicate, impeccably clad figure, uncompromisingly feminine in the roundness of its breasts and hips was nevertheless, Hope knew, as tough and finely tuned as a virtuoso's violin.

Alexa ran lightly out of her premises, noting the big black motor cycle parked up against the wall opposite her showroom window, its wing mirrors extended like insects' antennae. She told herself for the hundredth time not to be remotely curious about the fact that it was a highly expensive, prestigious piece of engineering. What Rick could afford was his own affair.

'Hi!' Rick said, straightening up from his polishing and smiling down into her eyes. He towered above her, his eyes piercingly blue and bright under his mane of thick blond hair.

Alexa was irritated to note that her heart-rate had increased.

'Good morning,' she said formally.

Rick's grin widened. He seemed to make the atmosphere around him shimmer and dance with energy. In his work-stained jeans, trainers, open shirt and body-warmer he was breathtakingly good-looking — even to Alexa, who was normally more impressed by rather serious-looking men in safe dark suits.

The Rover, which had been in a sorry and filthy state when it arrived on her premises, now gleamed and glinted like a freshly minted pound coin.

'You've worked wonders,' she told him stroking the bonnet appreciatively.

He raised amused eyebrows. 'Thanks!'

Alexa gave a little cough and patted her hair which fell in an exquisitively carved bob just below her ears. Rick had this disconcerting habit of seeming to be gently laughing at something — or someone. Surely not her. 'Can you manage to get the Golf Gti ready for a customer to see this afternoon?'

she asked, 'Oh — and Mrs Lake's Escort needs collecting from the paint shop and there's the baby seat to fit in the back.' She could feel the entrepreneurial adrenalin coursing through her veins as she spoke.

He smiled. 'No problem. Leave it all to me!'

She nodded briefly. She knew he would be totally reliable, wholly efficient.

She slipped deftly behind the wheel of her own silver Jaguar and started the engine.

On this shining spring morning, manoeuvring the softly purring car through the jumble of traffic, Alexa felt her usual warm surge of pleasure at being a fully contributing member to the thriving economy of this pretty Yorkshire town which had been her home for the last four years. Brought up in the urban sprawl of industrial South Yorkshire she had migrated to Arkenfield in the north of the county when the opportunity to purchase her business premises had given her the final spark of motivation needed to take the plunge and launch out fully on her own. Like many of life's important decisions, this resolve to cut adrift from her roots and her secure job as a personal secretary to the Managing Director of a car-hire firm in Sheffield had been prompted by the vagaries of chance. Her boss had invited her to one of his monthly Sunday lunchtime cocktail parties and she had become heavily engaged in conversation with an estate agent from York. On hearing of her interest in starting her own business and impressed with her knowledge of cars and the motor trade in general — which her job had given her the unique opportunity to acquire — he had told her of some premises on his books which were perfect for her needs and simply too good and cheap to miss. She had driven up to meet him the next weekend and they had toured the premises together. She knew immediately that a chance like this would not occur again. There was everything she needed — a large open-plan area on the ground floor which would make an ideal showroom, three rooms above for interviewing and administrative work and plenty of space at the back to put cars.

'It's perfect,' she had told the agent. ' — why so cheap? What's the snag?'

He had shrugged. 'It's been on the market too long. Run to seed. Local lads have broken in once or twice. The business people in the town just don't want to know — and that attitude is catching.'

Alexa's shrewd eye had recognised the potential in the building and the site. She had known immediately just what she wanted to do with it and local prejudice was no deterrent to her; she had seen the place with the fresh objective eye of an immigrant. 'I'll take it,' she had told him decisively.

As the Jaguar flowed smoothly down the High Street, Alexa reflected that things had turned out better than she could ever have dared hope. For not only had the business taken firm root and put out a number of healthy young branches, but she herself had become a part of this lively market town, was well accepted both professionally and socially. That gave her great satisfaction.

She looked down the length of the High Street at its comfortable jumble of the ancient and modern. At floor level there were glossy glass-fronted shops and banks, but above that the buildings retained their original character; pointed eaves, crooked little windows and uneven walls bearing witness to the architecture of years long gone by. She noticed a tiny iron-railed balcony, filled with boxes of flowers; waving sun-bright daffodils and military-erect tulips. They blazed coral and yellow against the vivid blue sky where white puffs of cloud cruised with lazy purposelessness. Happiness flooded through her, a deep warm glow of well-being.

'You look well, Alexa,' her accountant

commented. He gestured her to a chair and buzzed through to his secretary to bring coffee. 'I like punctuality,' he added in his blunt, Yorkshire manner. 'Very endearing quality.'

'Especially in a woman?' Alexa queried — a little defensively.

'Huh — ' Morris snorted, 'let's not get on to the war of the sexes issue. We've more serious things to think about than that — namely your balance sheet for the last year.' He held it reverentially in his hands. Alexa could see, from the expression on his face, that it was making very pleasant reading.

'Well, there's no need for me to tell you how well things are going, you know that. Lockton's of Arkenfield is well and truly thriving.'

'Yes,' she sighed. 'But what comes next? I'm reaching that difficult point, aren't I, when I need to grow and expand? It's no good standing still.'

He nodded. 'Yes.'

'But can I afford to, Morris?'

'You can't afford not to.' He laid the sheets on the desk, lit a thin cigar and looked steadily at her. Fragrant blue curls of smoke drifted into the air. 'Alexa, can I give you some general advice?'

'Yes, of course.'

'It strikes me, from a careful look at the figures, that whilst you started off with the intention of selling medium-price little hatchbacks to a mainly female market, what you are really best at is persuading wealthy men to part with large sums of money for prestige cars.'

'I don't persuade,' she countered with a bemused smile, for this aspect of her success never failed to mystify her. 'They just seem to buy them!'

'You create an atmosphere of competence and professionalism which combined with your female assets is a sure-fire winner,' he told her, sucking heavily on the cigar so that its tip sparkled and spat.

Alexa was silent for a moment

— slightly needled by his suggestion that her feminine charms were giving her a business advantage. 'You think I should concentrate on that side of things?' she asked evenly.

'I think you should expand in that area. Keep the small car business humming nicely as well.'

'That will mean extra staff, extra investment,' she said slowly.

He nodded.

'It also throws me well and truly into the arena with wealthy successful men, doesn't it. They'll be ninety-five per cent of the buyers.'

'That's no problem for you! You'll be a spectacular success. You're competent, astute, you've a sound business sense, you know how to handle people firmly — and you're tough. That's why Lockton's is thriving whilst similar outfits are going to the wall.'

Alexa was gratified, yet at the same time faintly troubled. He thinks I'm hard, she thought with a sudden revulsion against her competence and her professionalism. He thinks that if a woman is making her way in a traditionally male world then she's basically ruthless and uncaring about people. A hand of ice clutched at her heart. Am I getting to be like that she mused.

Morris, observing her worried expression and never dreaming for a moment that it was prompted by anything other than business concerns, said, 'Don't let this idea worry you. There's no rush. Things are fine for now. But we need to keep future years in mind; we'll talk this over in a month or so.'

She shook hands with him warmly. She knew that he always treated her with complete honesty, that he never treated her to soft words because he thought they were what she wanted to hear. I trust Morris, she told herself, easing the Jaguar out of its parking spot. In fact he's the only man I know whom I can fully trust. Except Royston of course she corrected herself hastily. She switched on the wipers. The yellow shiny morning had dissolved into a raw, thin white chill. Grey clouds hung above, swollen with rain.

Well naturally she trusted Royston. After all — she was going to marry him.

2

Royston was angry. As angry as his cool, controlled exterior would allow him at any rate.

They were dining at Alexa's flat, a graceful suite of rooms on the first floor of a small Victorian mansion which stood importantly in the middle of a truly old-fashioned garden on the north edge of Arkenfield. Alexa loved her flat, having nursed it through the chaos of kitchen and bathroom renovation, dry-rot killing and re-wiring. She hated to think of leaving it, had no intention to do so until she and Royston married — which was precisely the question at issue.

'Alexa, we must set a date for the wedding. People are beginning to wonder,' he said with solemn purpose.

Alexa fingered the diamonds on her left hand. 'I know darling, but we've only been engaged for a few months, there's no rush is there?' Being engaged was a pleasant state she thought. It meant that she was committed to a serious relationship so that other men did not pester her, yet at the same time she was a free agent, running her own life as she chose. She felt no desperate urge to be married. Not yet.

'Let's face it,' he said reasonably, 'I'm not as young as I used to be. I'm pushing forty. Time I settled down!' He smiled. It was a smile that held all the indulgence of one who has the undisputed advantage of age and experience. Royston Wentworth had joined his father's insurance broking company twenty years ago as a boy of eighteen. He knew all about the harsh cut and thrust of the financial business world. Alexa recalled Mr Wentworth senior telling her once with pride that she would do well to be guided by Royston in all business matters. What he didn't know on that score wasn't worth knowing. And Royston had indeed been very helpful as a guide and adviser. He handled all her insurances and his advice regarding the best guarantee plans to offer her customers when they bought a used car had been invaluable. It had enabled her to give the kind of faultless after-sales service that not only brought customers back a second time, but prompted them to recommend her warmly to friends and colleagues.

Alexa had approached Wentworth's Brokers at the very beginning of her business career. Her prospective account had caught Royston's interest and he had always dealt with it personally. Very gradually their occasional business discussions developed into lunch dates and then there were the dinner dances at Royston's golf club. His friends had been full of admiration for the attractive, poised young woman carving such a successful name for herself in the town and Royston had been proud to be her escort. An understanding that they would eventually marry began to take root and flower and it was no surprise to Alexa when Royston presented her with a splendid diamond cluster engagement ring for her Christmas present.

This evening, as usual, Royston was faultlessly elegant even in casual clothes. His brown hair, now greying at the temples, was neatly smoothed to frame his face whose classical features were resolute to the point of sternness. All in all he was the epitome of an attractive man in his prime. His friends and colleagues in the town certainly regarded him in that light and, moreover, viewed him as a supremely eligible bachelor who had so far eluded capture.

Alexa had a great respect for him and had always felt able to trust him completely. He was sober, impeccably honest and hard-working and a noted pillar of the local community, being on the committees of several social clubs and charitable organisations. His sense of humour was perhaps a little underdeveloped, but Alexa had never sought the company of hearty men who told vulgar jokes and brayed with masculine laughter. Royston was also, of course, totally sound financially — altogether a well-set-up, wholly dependable man.

He was regarding her intently. 'Now I've found you,' he persisted, 'why wait?'

She sighed inwardly. 'Yes, I do see what you mean.'

'And there's no problem about money,' he commented practically. 'I can easily support a wife and family — whether my wife works or not.' He smiled with satisfaction. 'There's absolutely no need to delay things.'

'I don't need supporting,' she murmured, reflecting on her own financial status, which was remarkably healthy for a woman in her mid twenties who had started with virtually nothing four years before.

'I know that, dear. Don't let's argue about it. I'm immensely proud of you and your business and it will be wonderful to have a wife with her own money. Some of the directors' wives do nothing but race around in fancy cars running up huge bills at expensive dress shops. My God — the money they get through!'

'Oh dear,' she said softly.

'But of course, darling,' he continued seriously, 'if you ever wanted to give up work I'd be only too happy to provide for you — very handsomely. Don't think I'd begrudge the money.'

The prospect seemed to give him considerable pleasure Alexa noted — and for the very first time in their relationship a cool hand of doubt slid its icy fingers around her heart. She wondered, with a sting of alarm, whether it was just possible that she and Royston were making a terrible mistake. Perhaps they were not as truly suited to each other as she had always thought. 'Maybe — deep down — that's the kind of wife you want, Royston,' she mused, 'the kind who spends money rather than makes it.'

'Oh heavens, what on earth are you

talking about?' He swept a stray lock of hair impatiently from his forehead. 'I've no intention of getting into a discussion like that!' He gave her a long look. 'You're so touchy these days. What's the matter?'

A chill ran down Alexa's spine. Yes, she was touchy — but it only seemed to happen when she was with Royston. At work she was fine. And at present there wasn't much time for anything else. Poor Royston. Was she neglecting him in the same way that men building businesses neglect their wives and girl friends? With quiet resolve she went to sit down beside him on the sofa, curling up her slim legs in their brown velvet jeans and kicking off her shoes. Royston slid an arm around her, feeling her small, slender body warm and pliant against his own under the silky raspberry-pink blouse. She really was a catch, he thought. Some of his long-married friends were wild with envy. 'You're not letting the business get on top of you are you?' he said severely as she nestled into him.

'No.' She spoke calmly. 'I'm busy — but everything's going fine.' They sat in silence, staring into the fire which burned with the spruce logs Alexa kept on order from the local timber merchant — a Jaguar enthusiast whom she had already supplied with several cars. It was quite true that everything was going fine with the business. Demand and turnover were steadily increasing. Never before had trading been so challenging, so exhilarating, such wonderful fun. Repeat business from satisfied customers coupled with a steady increase in new business was creating a noticeable snowball effect.

Very soon she would be forced to make radical changes. But just at the moment her time at work was offering such a depth of satisfaction that the rest of her life seemed to pale into insignificance. The atmosphere of the place was so happy these days, especially since the arrival of Rick Markland!

Rick's boundless zest for life and exuberant merriness rubbed off on everyone who came into contact with him. Simply thinking about him sent tendrils of warmth curling around Alexa's heart. So why, she mused, given that things were going so well in the business, why then was she so often on edge with Royston? Could it be that for a woman, real pressure of work and job satisfaction were incompatible with the flowering of romance and emotional attachment? No — she refused to have anything to do with that notion.

'Let's get one or two provisional dates pencilled in,' Royston said briskly, sitting up and pulling a slim leather diary from his pocket. He flicked over the pages. 'How about September or October. An autumn wedding — that could be nice?'

'Mmn,' she murmured, wishing that he would kiss her instead of being so efficient.

'Well,' he glanced at her, 'does that give you time to get everything done? I know how it is. You beautiful young ladies; you need time to see to all the new clothes and so on.'

'Yes,' she agreed meekly, startled to discover that the idea of new clothes elicited only the faintest spark of interest at present. She felt quite opposed to being pinned down on dates this evening. She wanted to relax, to be cherished and made to feel womanly and wanted. She put her face up to Royston's and pressed her lips softly to his. Royston was pleasant to kiss. His mouth always tasted fresh and minty and he was never too insistent, never out of control — an approach which suited Alexa perfectly. The idea of wild passion had always alarmed her; that would involve a lot of letting go; would entail exposing the rawness of her sexual nature which she had never been prepared to acknowledge fully. She felt, on the whole, that wild passion was something she could do without.

He kissed her obligingly for a few moments, then disentangled himself.

'You're still evading the issue,' he said heavily, reaching for the diary which had slipped to the carpet.

She sighed and rested her head against the pile of soft silk cushions.

Royston's face darkened. 'Alexa! Is it *you* that is having doubts? Don't you really want to marry me. Is that it?'

She was shocked, sat up with a jerk. 'No — of course that's not it. Oh Royston — please; I'm just tired that's all.'

'Is it,' he persisted grimly, 'is there someone else? Is that the problem?'

She gaped at him incredulously. 'No! How could you think that?'

'You've changed,' he said flatly. 'This last month or two you've become evasive, you won't make decisions, you're always too tired to discuss important things — like our wedding,' he finished meaningfully.

'Royston — darling, I'm working flat out. We're all tired!'

'We?' he queried coldly.

'All the staff.'

'Oh I see. They come before me do they?'

'No, of course not — but my work is important.'

'Yes, I'm beginning to wonder if that's the sort of competition I can't handle. I think I could deal with a flesh and blood rival — but your business might be just too much to swallow.'

With horror she watched him button his jacket, get out his car keys, prepare to leave. She was appalled and baffled by this sudden turn of events, as though their relationship which had always cruised along so smoothly had taken a sharp nose dive and embedded itself firmly in the mud.

'Oh darling — please don't go. Sit down and have a brandy.' Her eyes were full of anxiety.

He hesitated and considered relenting.

'Please,' she cajoled.

'Well all right.' He settled again on the sofa. 'I'm sorry I was angry, I just get the feeling that you're never going to commit yourself.' He waved his diary at her with mocking admonishment. 'So, how about it? I'll catch you while the iron is hot,' he said, with a horrible mixing of metaphors.

Alexa swallowed down all her fatigue. Her head seemed to be swimming in a whirl of confused thoughts and feelings. The last thing she was ready for was making an important decision. But Royston was already ringing two dates in his diary and somehow she could not find the heart or strength to stop him.

* * *

There was a particularly difficult problem to deal with — the proverbially awkward customer. Alexa thought that she would pay him a visit. She decided to take Rick along. She had noticed that her customers liked and trusted him and that he had an ability to adapt himself to their individual idiosyncrasies. She had also noted, with admiration, that he was a shrewd judge of character.

He sized people up quickly and could spot a time-wasting customer a mile off — skills she possessed too, but had acquired rather painfully over a span of time. She called to him from the door of her office. She could hear him downstairs in the showroom humming to himself as he worked. She smiled, knowing that he would be doing a thorough job. When Rick had checked a car she could be sure that every one of its irritating little faults would have been identified.

'Rick, can you spare me a minute?'

Immediately the humming stopped and he came flying up the stairs, eyes shining, hair winging in all directions. She smiled. He was so good to have around, he made the atmosphere glow — always grinning, always friendly, forever hurtling up and down her stairs with unflagging energy.

'Hi there, Miss Lockton — for you I could spare a lifetime!' He stood looking down at her, his thumbs hooked into the pockets of his jeans, a wedge of mane falling roguishly over one eye and the sunniest of smiles on his face.

Alexa felt slightly overwhelmed — as she sometimes did with Rick. He had such tremendous presence. And he was so tall, so broad, so supple. He combined the strength of a rugby forward with the swift deftness of a wing three-quarter. The sheer bigness of him was . . . well — exciting she supposed. Alarmed at this fresh discovery she retreated into her room and sat behind the defence lines of the desk, her conker coloured hair falling in a silky gleam over the black-and-white silk blouse with its high round collar and big pussy-cat bow.

Rick followed, sniffing appreciatively at the cloud of Diorella she left in her wake. His eyes rested on her with interest.

'Sit down, Rick.' She gestured gracefully to a chair.

'Oh dear — this seems serious. Have I done something terrible?' he joked.

'No, not at all.' She smiled at him,

warmed as usual by his presence, his consistent good humour. 'Can you leave everything and come with me to see a customer? I might have to bring his car back here, so I'll need a spare driver.'

'Sure I can leave everything,' he grinned, 'for a morning out with you I'd pass up Princess Diana!'

She regarded him with indulgent chiding. 'This is a business trip and it might be a tricky one. Just be serious and behave yourself!'

'Do I ever let you down in front of the customers,' he asked mockingly. 'Don't I always act with commendable respect and sobriety?'

'Yes you do,' she smiled, noting not for the first time, his skill with words. She wondered why he was not in a job which made more use of those skills. She buzzed through to the next door office. 'Hope, will you bring through the Armitage account?'

Hope appeared almost instantly and laid a slim buff folder on Alexa's desk.

‘Morning, Rick — how’s things?’ she asked.

Rick leapt to his feet and swept plump little Hope off the ground in a great, exuberant bear hug. ‘Things are simply fantastic — as they always are since I came to work in this wonderful emporium of female beauty and talent!’

‘Aah!’ Hope sighed fervently, ‘if only I were twenty years younger.’

She patted his cheek and wriggled to the ground.

‘Who’s counting?’ Rick grinned.

‘I am, unfortunately,’ Hope returned, ‘all the way up to the sad conclusion that there’s a generation gap between us!’

‘Help — mothers are certainly getting younger and sexier these days if that’s the case,’ Rick told her.

‘When you two have quite finished.’ Alexa interposed calmly, ‘I think it’s time we set off. We may be a couple of hours, Hope. Can you manage?’

‘Of course I can — and knowing Mr Armitage I think I’ll have the stiff brandies waiting when you get back.'

'So what's the trouble with the Armitage guy?' Rick asked as Alexa guided the Jaguar through the flow of traffic along Arkenfield's High Street.

'He bought a car a year ago,' she explained, 'a top of the range Rover Vitesse with only seven thousand miles on the clock. He's been through a complete set of shock absorbers, a master cylinder on the clutch, a pair of carburettors and new brake pipes.'

Rich whistled, 'Wow — sounds like he's given it quite a pounding!'

'That's exactly what I thought — except I suspect the pounding comes from his eighteeen-year-old son who likes to borrow the car in the evenings and impress his girl friends.'

'Uh-huh — a bit of a raver is he?'

'You might say that,' Alexa agreed. 'The car was covered for all these things on its warranty agreement, although the insurance people started getting a little cross when we put in the last claim!'

‘I’ll bet they did!’

‘But now the warranty has expired and Mr Armitage is demanding a new gear box — to be suppled and fitted at my expense.’

‘Is he now? That seems like a tall order,’ Rick grinned.

‘Quite. He’s not getting it of course. That’s what we’re going to tell him.’ She gave a grim little smile.

‘Sounds like fun!’ Rick rubbed his hands gleefully.

Out on the A1, Alexa put her foot down and revelled in the Jaguar’s smooth surge of power. Cars and lorries labouring up the slow lane slipped back into the distance. ‘I love this car,’ she remarked spontaneously, ‘it gains me a lot of road respect. People think twice about arguing with it.’

‘I wouldn’t have thought you needed a big car to gain respect,’ Rick replied reflectively, ‘you seem to do perfectly well on your own merits.’

‘Sometimes, Rick, people feel very small and frightened underneath — even successful business ladies.' Her light tone belied the depth of feeling behind the words. She frowned. How was it she had been prompted to make such a revealing comment to this man who was virtually a stranger.

Rick declined to expand on her theme. He stretched out in his seat, relaxed but watchful. His eyes slid across to Alexa, noting that the morning sunlight had thrown a haze of fire around her chestnut hair.

He smiled. 'And this is work!' he exclaimed blissfully.

'You seem to be enoying yourself,' Alexa smiled in return.

'Yeah — I certainly am!'

'So am I. I don't usually — not with male passengers.'

'You're joking!'

'I'm not joking. Some of them make me as jumpy as hell!'

'*You* — jumpy!'

'Yes.' A note of warning sounded at the back of Alexa's head. She was doing it again, sharing her private thoughts with Rick. She never discussed these feminist kinds of issues with anyone except her female friends. Why she should open up to Rick Markland of all people was quite incomprehensible. And she did not think it was very wise on reflection.

'What do they do to make you jumpy?' he asked with interest.

'Oh — you wouldn't understand — you're a man after all. How could you?'

'Hey that's not fair! Come on, tell me. What am I not doing that all the rest of them do? I really want to know!'

Her eyes twinkled. 'They sit forward and they look round anxiously at road junctions and they move their feet as though there was a brake pedal in front of them, and they tell you when it's clear to overtake and . . . '

'Don't go on. It's too horrible. I believe you. What a rotten lot we guys are.'

She laughed. Suddenly it all seemed

quite trivial and no more than mildly amusing.

'Well,' he said, 'looks like I've passed the model male passenger test. Are there any more hurdles to jump?'

'Yes, you can drop the 'Miss Lockton' and call me Alexa.'

'Oh — I've earned that privilege have I?' he mocked.

'With the quality of your work and with your commitment.'

'Thank you,' he said simply. 'I thought at first that you disapproved of me.'

'No,' she shook her head, keeping a careful eye on her wing mirror as the Jaguar raced past car carriers and petrol tankers. 'No — it's just that you have a different way of behaving, a different approach to things from anyone I've come across before.'

'Oh — like what?'

'Like saying what you think,' she smiled.

'Being honest you mean?'

'Yes — I suppose that's it.'

'Anything else?' he probed.

‘Mmn — let’s see.’ She mused a little sucking in her lips and trying to be serious. ‘Well, there’s the matter of flirting outrageously with Hope — and with all the female customers.’

‘They like it,’ he said flatly.

‘The fact had not escaped me,’ she returned in dry tones.

‘I’d very much like to flirt with you too,’ he said teasingly, ‘but I don’t think you’d approve!’

‘Of course not,’ she said correctly, glad that she was driving and did not have to face the interrogating glance of his sharp blue eyes. She felt a sudden warmth lapping up into her cheeks. ‘That would be quite inappropriate. After all — I am the ‘boss lady’ to coin a phrase of yours.’

‘Quite,’ he said with lavish reverence.

There was a silence between them; only the engine’s powerful throbbing purr to be heard. The rolling Yorkshire fields spread themselves to east and west, carefully demarcated by stone walling so that they resembled some giant chequer-board. A flock of game birds rose up suddenly into the air — a dark moving arch, dipping and gliding then swooping down to settle again like some vast living sickle laid over the neatly tilled ground. In the distance, the hills stretched up against the sky, row upon row like tightly clenched knuckles, eventually softening to a dark azure line on the horizon.

Alexa said softly, 'I should remind you Rick that I am planning to get married soon. Flirting with anyone is strictly out of the question.'

'Oh yes,' Rick observed drily, 'the guy with the grey suits and the matching grey face who comes to collect you sometimes.'

Alexa felt her features freeze into immobility. Her heart thudded painfully with amazed anger that Rick should dare to make such a comment about Royston and also with a deep and horrible suspicion that it was cruelly and terrifyingly accurate.

'Don't ever say anything like that

about my fiancé again,' she flared at him. 'You're my employee. My private life has absolutely nothing to do with you. Your opinion is not required. Do I make myself clear?'

Rick smiled gently, apparently unabashed. 'Yes,' he said, 'unfortunately you do — otherwise I might say plenty more!'

'Rick!' she snapped warningly, her hand gripping the steering-wheel tightly, 'you're going too far.'

He sighed. 'I know my place,' he said, 'a very low and humble one. Relax, I'll be a good boy — like I promised you.' He gave his deep merry laugh, refused to look in the least chastened and began to hum softly to himself.

* * *

Joe Armitage was a prosperous dairy farmer who called a spade a spade and wasted no time on the little niceties of life which oil the social wheels. Dispensing with any form of greeting he grunted to Alexa to follow him through to the back yard where his car was parked. He strode off, leaving her to pick her way across the thickly muddied track which formed his driveway and led into the cobbled yard flanked by buildings of local weathered stone. She cursed herself silently for not having foreseen the inevitably messy conditions on Armitage's farm, noting that her dainty Charles Jourdan shoes were quite unsuitable and already soaked.

Rick loped along behind. 'If only I had Walter Raleigh's cloak, I'd throw it down,' he chuckled quietly.

Alexa skidded slightly. Instantly Rick's hand was there to steady her, large and solid and reassuring. She clung on momentarily.

'O.K.?' he queried.

'Yes.' She was truly glad of his presence.

'Well,' Armitage said heavily coming to a halt beside a large car thickly encrusted with mud so that its original soft metallic green paint could be barely detected, 'there it is. It's caused me more damn bother than all the other cars I've had put together!' He threw the offending vehicle a look of deep dislike then transferred his gaze to Alexa. 'So what are you going to do about it?'

She smiled at him calmly, refusing to take up the aggressive challenge.

'It's nice to see you again, Mr Armitage,' she said evenly. 'I've brought along my assistant, Rick Markland,' she added politely, noting Armitage's eyes rest with a certain curious admiration on Rick's impressive figure.

'Good,' Armitage said sourly, 'you'll be needing a spare driver. You'll have to take the car back with you. It's high time it got sorted out good and proper.'

'Mr Armitage,' Alexa replied patiently, 'it's always unfortunate when a car has a run of faults. However I'm sure you will agree that on each occasion the fault was cured, without any delay — and with no cost to you.'

'Inconvenience,' he grumbled.

Alexa shook her head. 'No,' she said reasonably, 'I always sent another car for you to use whilst yours was being repaired. There was no inconvenience.'

Mr Armitage, briefly at a loss for words, was saved further embarrassment by the arrival of his son — a big lumbering lad who strolled across to survey the scene at leisure.

'Is she taking it back then,' he asked his father, 'having another go at putting it right?' He looked at Alexa with silent, insolent relish, obviously anticipating a little fun.

He's a latter day bear-baiter, Alexa thought grimly, resolving not to be cast in the leading bear role.

Armitage muttered inaudibly.

Rick fixed an unswerving, appraising eye on the youth and Alexa noted a flicker of discomfort move over the brash features.

'Will you just start the car up, Mr Armitage,' Alexa asked, 'Let me have a listen to it?'

'Oh — bit of a mechanic are you?' he jeered.

'No, but it's useful to know what the problem seems to be.'

He got in, Alexa joining him in the passenger seat. Rick wandered across to the lad who was fondling a gleaming new motor-bike with appreciation.

'It sounds O.K.,' Alexa ventured as the Rover roared into life.

'Gears are sticking,' Armitage growled.

She invited him to move the car out of the driveway and along the little road which snaked around the farm. She noted the insistent wink of the oil warning light, but there seemed to be no other real problem.

As they parked again in the yard Alexa said, 'I think you should check the oil level Mr Armitage, before we go any further.'

'What?' he roared. 'What the hell has that got to do with it?'

Alexa was pretty sure now that there was nothing wrong with the car beyond a little neglect and rough handling and that the main problem was Mr Armitage's spoiled son who wondered how far he could go to amuse himself by causing trouble whilst his father took most of the aggravation. She sighed inwardly, anticipating a lengthy and ugly scene.

'Haven't you noticed the oil warning light?' she asked politely.

'Never bother with all them instruments — like a bloomin' cockpit. Barry's the one who deals with all that. Come here,' he shouted to his son, 'I want you!'

Barry came across the yard and faced his father with a sulky grimace, suspecting trouble.

'What about the oil in this car?' Armitage hissed.

'Eh?' the lad stared.

'When did you last put some oil in?' his father barked.

Rick intervened. 'Barry tells me he likes to do a bit of hard driving — top-speed stuff. Uses up a bit of oil doesn't it, that sort of thing?' he suggested reasonably.

Alexa could see that Rick's probing gaze had unnerved the lad, delved into the well guarded fortress of his conscience and unearthed a spark of guilt. 'Well, anyone can forget!' he muttered defiantly.

Rick had opened up the bonnet, was examining the dipstick. 'It's really quite dangerously low,' he murmured. 'I've seen cars seize up completely if they run dry.' He winked at Alexa letting her know that he was laying things on rather thick. He turned and eyed the lad sternly.

Barry looked to his father for support, his face flushed with confusion.

'What is this,' he demanded pettishly, 'a flaming inquisition?'

Armitage looked at Rick, then at his son. He was beginning to see the light. 'You told me the gears were stiff,' he yelled at the lad, 'you told me the car was no good — and all the time you were just running around in it never doing a blasted thing to maintain it. You've been playing silly games and making me look a damned fool.' He jerked his head dismissively. 'Get out of my sight!'

The lad slunk off, glancing up at Rick with a mingle of admiration and resentment.

Alexa felt that this was an advantageous moment to bring the interview to a close. 'I don't think there's anything further I can do at present,' she said with untroubled firmness. 'Get in touch straight away if you have any more trouble — and do keep the oil topped up. It is important!'

'Damn kids,' Armitage grumbled, 'cause bother from the day they're born. You've had a wasted journey,' he told Alexa as she walked back to her Jaguar — which was as near an apology as he was going to offer.

'I'm glad everything's all right,' she said diplomatically.

'Well look,' Armitage said in conciliatory tones as she started the engine, 'I'll probably change the Rover soon — perhaps you'd look out for something suitable — low mileage — nice condition, you know the sort of thing. Jag like this one might be nice.'

Alexa smiled. 'Leave it with me; I'll be in touch as soon as I find something.'

As she turned back onto the south-bound carriageway of the A1 Rick said, 'I'd really like to see you make a tidy profit out of that guy. He deserves to be thrown to the sharks!'

'I'm no shark!' Alexa laughed.

'No you're not. You're a true professional; was I impressed!'

'Really,' she said with a warm stab of delight. This was genuine praise, there was no hint of male flattery, no suggestion of patronage.

'That's not to say that I wouldn't have liked to wring the guy's neck for treating you like he did.' She saw that his fists were clenched so the knuckles showed white.

'Come on Rick — I'm no Dresden

China lady. I can handle difficult customers — awkward ones, rude ones. That's my job. I'm good at looking after myself you know.'

'Are you?' he asked intently.

'Yes, of course. I'm used to it. You don't think I need protecting from my customers do you?' she laughed.

'I think you need a little gentle looking after,' he said in a low voice, causing her heart to thump momentarily, 'After all when even the toughest guy gets home after a hard day there's a nice lady to give him some tender care — but you . . . '

'I've got a guy,' she reminded him sweetly.

Rick was silent. Alexa could see from the corner of her eye the muscles of his jaw working.

'You were enormously helpful Rick,' she said softly. 'You came in at just the right moment with just the right approach. I was very grateful; I'd resigned myself to a protracted and unpleasant interview.'

He pressed his lips together. 'Thanks,' he said.

'In fact,' she mused, 'we were rather a good double act!'

'Yeah,' Rick drawled, 'I reckon we could make a very good double act, professional — and otherwise!'

Alexa swallowed hard. She knew that Rick was making a sexual implication and the mere thought of it filled her with an intensity of wild excitement she had never experienced before. She was painfully aware of his animal masculinity beside her, the broad chest, lean and tightly muscled under the thin T-shirt, the powerful thighs encased in hugging denim, the great strong forearms dappled with the mid-day sunlight and rugged with a mass of shiny blond hairs. All this she was rawly sensitive of, even with her eyes on the road ahead. She knew that if she were to turn and look at him full face, allow those rakish blue eyes to burn mockingly into her and the wide firm mouth to smile invitingly she would feel as though hot liquid were being poured down her spine and a trembling weakness would develop somewhere in the region of her calves. It had begun to happen rather regularly when Rick was around. She knew it was just a passing phase and she also knew that to get involved with her handsome employee would be insane. 'Rick, as you insist on flirting — let's just keep it on a nice light level shall we?' she said casually.

There was a pause. 'It wasn't flirting,' he said in a low voice.

She held her breath.

'But I really did overstep the mark that time. I'm sorry.' He gave a heavy sigh.

'It's quite O.K. Please don't worry about it at all,' she said brightly in the tone of a kindly headmistress.

Neither of them knew what to say next. A constraint grew between them. Alexa felt a crushing disappointment. She had been enjoying herself so much in his company and now it was all spoiled. Damn!

'You know I've never met a woman like you Alexa,' he said out of the blue. 'There's only one other woman I know who's anywhere near as remarkable.'

'Really — who's that?'

'My grandmother.'

Alexa smiled. 'Oh — should I be flattered?'

'Yes — she's terrific!'

Alexa breathed deeply and took a firm grip on herself. 'Rick, it's very nice of you to be so complimentary. I really do appreciate it — but I don't think you should.'

'Why?' He gave a lazily sardonic smile. 'There's nothing wrong with being complimentary. OK, I admit I shouldn't have criticised your guy or hinted that we'd have a great time together in bed. But I've a perfect right to tell you how much I admire you — and I don't intend to stop!'

Alexa felt she was rapidly losing control of the situation. No man had ever talked to her about being 'great in bed'. Not even Royston. Certainly not

Royston. She couldn't imagine it.

Colour burned in her cheeks. 'Please Rick, stop it. Please!' she said in a tight voice. She leaned over quickly and snapped on the radio.

A great burst of violins surged from the car's four speakers.

'Vivaldi,' Rick said. 'Great stuff!'

'Heavens, you were quick to recognise it. Do you like classical music?' she asked curiously.

'Yeah — among other things,' he grinned. 'I'm a bit of a musical maverick. Like to try anything that turns up!'

They listened with that special enjoyment that comes of a true sharing of taste. Royston tolerated rather than enjoyed classical music — but here was Rick tapping his feet enthusiastically and singing along with 'The Four Seasons' with all the exuberance of the kids on 'Top of the Pops'. Alexa allowed herself to join in. Happiness bubbled up inside her.

That evening she stayed on to catch

up on the paper-work which mounted up alarmingly when she was out of the office. Hope had left a neatly stacked pile of documents for her to check and sign and she started to go through them methodically. As usual she forgot the time and was amazed to notice that it was past eight when she checked her watch prior to collecting her things and locking up. She went down the stairs and through into the showroom. With shock she saw three youths standing in the doorway, silent and grinning. She cursed herself for forgetting to lock the outer door whilst she worked upstairs.

'Can I help you?' she asked automatically.

'Shouldn't be surprised,' one said with an ugly, menacing leer. 'Got some nice stuff 'ere 'aven't you, Missis?' He stroked the shining bonnet of a two-year-old silver Mercedes she had bought in the day before. 'Very nice indeed.' He got out a small knife and made a minute scratch on the car's glossy wing. Alexa swallowed. Fear clutched at her stomach. 'I think you'd better leave,' she said calmly.

'No chance. We've come a long way — on us bikes. Don't wanna go yet. We come to Arkenfield for special fun. No-one knows us here you see.' He spoke with the insolent authority of a ring leader.

His companions smiled obligingly.

'What do you want?' Alexa asked, outwardly quite composed but inwardly sick with apprehension.

'Just a bit o' fun. Nothing much!' He made another scratch. 'Get going lads,' he instructed the minions, 'Nice bit of art work on these classy cars. The well-off gits who buy 'em might really appreciate it!'

They advanced into the showroom and surveyed the shining cars with gleeful anticipation. Alexa stood fixed to the spot, wondering what on earth to do next.

Then miraculously, to her surprise and heartfelt relief, she saw Rick Markland's large frame appear in the doorway. He too had been working late.

With the stealthy purpose of a panther he positioned himself behind the unsuspecting ring-leader. Alexa watched with fascination as Rick put his hands under the youth's armpits and lifted him with ease into the air so that his legs dangled like a stuffed puppet. 'Having fun sonny?' Rick enquired, shaking the lad and making his head bob about uselessly. With a sudden swift movement he transferred the lad over his shoulder like a sack of coal, landed some resounding blows on his bottom then carried him to the door and deposited him in the road. 'Don't call again sunshine,' he said cheerfully, 'I wouldn't like to get really cross!'

The two hangers-on watched the humiliation of their leader with wide-eyed amazement. As Rick advanced on them their eyes curdled with fear.

'Out!' Rick barked. They were already on their way. Rick shut the door firmly behind them as they slunk away down the street. 'Well,' he said, moving across to Alexa, 'I don't think they'll be back.'

'No,' she agreed faintly.

'You didn't want me to keep them here — ring the police and so on?' he queried, looking into her troubled face.

'No. Oh no. Let's hope they think twice before trying it again.' She sighed. 'They were just kids weren't they?'

'Hey — don't go all soft. I let them off pretty lightly!'

She smiled. 'Yes — I'm glad you did.'

'I thought you'd have been full of indignation about the presumption of the male sex,' he grinned, 'taking advantage of a poor helpless woman!'

His jokey tone raised no more than a weak smile from her. 'I've had lads a bit like them working for me in the past. Some of them had rotten lives — parents out of work or always drinking, no spare money, crowded homes like rabbit warrens. Terrible!' She gave a rueful, shaky smile.

Rick stared down at her, his eyes full of tenderness. 'I can't think of one person in a hundred who'd be so forgiving,' he said in a low voice, 'given what those lads must have made you feel.'

'Yes,' she passed a trembling hand across her forehead. The shock was just beginning to seep in. 'They made me feel pretty bad.'

'Hey!' Rick said with concern, 'are you O.K.?'

She turned her face to his, her eyes liquid and dark in a white face. She felt the depth of his solicitude as he gazed down at her. The showroom was hushed and still now but brilliantly lit under the spotlights which came on automatically in the evening. Never had Alexa felt Rick's presence so forcefully. It was as though his eyes were burning down into the heart of her. She moistened her lips with her tongue and exuded a soft sighing breath. The atmosphere was electric and quivering with tension as though they were wired up together and a current was flowing between them.

For seconds neither of them moved, then with tender authority Rick pushed her away from the glare of the lights into the darkness of the stair-well beyond. He placed his arms around her and held her securely. 'It's all right now,' he whispered reassuringly, 'it's all O.K.'

She felt the protection of his strong, hard body and rested gratefully against him. They held each other, perfectly still, perfectly silent. Then slowly his hands began to move across her back in a very different kind of caress.

She trembled. 'No Rick, no!' she moaned, knowing what was going to happen, knowing that she would be powerless to resist it.

'Yes,' he murmured, 'it was inevitable. It had to happen sooner or later — there's nothing to be afraid of.' He bent his head to hers and laid his mouth on her lips.

Alexa sighed. Impulsively she threw her arms around his neck in total abandonment, clinging to him and drinking him in, savouring the smell of his skin, the taste of his tongue. Sheer delight ripped through her body. She thrust her tongue hungrily into the warm darkness of his mouth, suddenly wild with an intensity of desire she had never experienced before. His big, gentle hands caressed her shoulder blades and massaged the base of her neck with exquisite sensitivity. Her own hands had found their way inside his T-shirt and were travelling over the satiny smooth skin of his back, marvelling at the deep, solid, living warmth of him. The connection between them was of such violent, electric force that she felt she would faint from sheer pleasure.

Yet still she retained the strength to know that she should protest. There was still enough resolve for her mouth to utter the words of restraint — 'Rick, no, please you mustn't.' But all the time her heart was saying yes, yes, yes. His tongue seemed to know everything about her mouth as though he had kissed her to perfection many times before, as though he was reaching down into her soul. She pressed herself into him, her voice repeating over and over, 'Rick, darling, darling, darling!'

He linked his arms beneath her buttocks and lifted her up against him. She opened her eyes, heavy and drugged with desire now and gazed at him. His glance burned into her. 'My love,' he breathed huskily, 'I want you so much. I want to make love to you — for ever and ever!'

His words brought her to her senses with a shock. 'Rick, let me go,' she begged, 'please let me go!' Her big eyes were wide with horror, realising all the implications of the amazing events of the last few moments.

He allowed her to slide down gently over his body, then placed his hands on her shoulders. 'I've always had girls before,' he said hoarsely, 'but you're a woman — a sophisticated, sensual, sensitive woman. I shall never want anyone else.'

'Rick. You mustn't say these things. It's madness!' She raised stricken eyes to his face.

'No, I shouldn't. But I've never been

a man to stay within the confines of what should and shouldn't be. And I'm not starting now!' he finished with uncharacteristic roughness.

'Rick, for God's sake,' she pleaded, rational thought flooding back, 'I'm going to be married soon.'

'So you keep telling me,' he said shortly. 'Perhaps you'd like to remind me as well that I'm your employee — just a hired hand.'

'I'm not that petty,' she retorted angrily.

His eyes blazed down. 'No, you're not,' he agreed. 'You're the least petty woman I've ever met — and I mean that from the bottom of my heart. You're truly wonderful and precious — and I've no intention of letting you throw yourself away on that grey-faced guy!'

Alexa gasped. She raised her hand and struck him hard on the cheek.

He took it unflinchingly.

'You bastard,' she burst out. 'Do you think you can just gather me up into your arms, sweep me literally off my feet, give me a few kisses and expect me to drop a man I've known for years; a reliable, serious, truly good man, whom I trust and respect? Drop him just like that? You must be crazy.' She paused, at a loss to say more.

His eyes glinted. 'Have you said all you want?' he asked.

'What more is there to say? I would have thought the issue was quite simple!' Her heart beat with furious emotion against her rib cage.

'Oh yes — I'm sure the issue is very simple indeed. I've something to say too. A woman who truly loves her man doesn't kiss another one like you just kissed me. So don't fool yourself, Alexa.' He gave an ironic smile. 'Of course she might well hit the man she *really* loves if she's passionate and angry!' He slid her a quizzical glance.

He's telling me I love him, Alexa thought in total bewilderment at what was happening. She covered her eyes with her hand. Suddenly she felt utterly drained and weary. 'Oh God, this whole conversation is pure madness,' she murmured in despair. 'I must go home now. Please let me go Rick,' she asked, noticing that his hand still lay heavily on her shoulder.

He gave a shuddering sigh, then released her. His harsh urgency melted suddenly away to be replaced by the habitual, casual cheerfulness. 'Are you all right now?' He brushed her cheek lightly with his finger. 'Feel O.K. to go home on your own?'

'Oh yes,' she said hastily, the thought of his accompanying her home stirring up a positive hornet's nest of emotions, 'I'm absolutely fine.'

'Come on, I'll see you to your car.' He spoke in friendly tones as though nothing of importance had happened.

Settled in the driver's seat she felt calmer. She pressed a button and the window slid down with a soft whirr. Glancing gratefully up at him, she said softly, 'Thank you Rick, I don't know what I'd have done if you hadn't been there.' She recalled the leering youths with a shudder.

He grinned, then gazed down at her for a long moment. 'I'm glad I was around to take care of you,' he said, his voice low and gentle, 'You really do need that and I'm just the one to do it!'

A small electric spark of shock stabbed in Alexa's chest. She started the engine and revved it with grim determination. She did not want to be sucked back into the swirling emotional vortex. 'Good night Rick. I think you'll find that I'm generally rather good at looking after myself.' Her tone was firmly dismissive and she was already pressing the button to raise the window.

His hand held it firmly down and the mechanism clicked and whirred in useless protest. 'Oh I know I'm a rank outsider, I've all the odds against me,' he said enigmatically, 'but there's still a chance. You're not married yet!'

He released the window, gave the roof of the Jaguar a friendly slap then vaulted swiftly on to his bike and was gone.

3

A kiss! So what! She could handle it!

Nothing in life was straightforward and this evening's events had merely been one of those banana skins fate tosses in one's path from time to time. She had skidded, but she was not going to fall. So Alexa told herself determinedly as she broke eggs into a bowl in preparation for a mushroom omelette. The liquid swirled and frothed in response to the whizzing blades of the hand blender. She had realised for some time now that Rick Markland's presence had a disturbing effect on her, despite all her fine and firm resolutions to remain immune to his magic. She had been prepared to accept it for what it was — some inexplicable and irrational phenomenon of little substance that would melt away like a child's sand castle in the inevitable swirl of the tide. She remembered this dizzy feeling happening before, just once, when she was fifteen and had been wildly attracted to the captain of the school's cricket team. He too had been a big powerful blond. She smiled at the recollection which brought with it nothing but happy feelings.

But now she was grown-up and well able to deal with these little pieces of grit which lodged in life's machinery from time to time. Being in business had taught her that every problem had a number of possible solutions if one only takes the trouble to think them carefully through. One reassuring course of action now would be to ring Royston — but unfortunately, tonight was his squash night. Royston took his sport seriously — and at very regular intervals: squash on Tuesdays, golf practice on Sunday mornings, matches on Wednesday afternoons. He liked to think of himself as matching any younger man for speed and fitness.

She slipped a wedge of butter into the cast-iron omelette pan and began to slice the mushrooms with swift, deft strokes. Her knife paused for a moment over the wooden chopping-board. She wondered how Rick would be feeling now. Would he experience regret about his behaviour? Perhaps he would even feel obliged to leave. Please God he doesn't, she thought with horror. I'll never manage without him; things are so busy. He really is an indispensable asset in the day-to-day running of things — and I'd miss him like hell, she concluded with a quivering thrill of realisation. She stood quite still, caught up in her thoughts, unable to stop herself reliving those moments of warmth and connection with this man who had simply walked in from the streets into her life just a few short weeks ago.

The smell of acrid smoke jarred her back into reality. Spiralling black curls poured in fury from the omelette pan. In alarm she threw open the window and thrust the pan and its contents onto the stone sill outside. The smoke cruised away into the distance and the sweet dusk atmosphere stole into the kitchen. The April evening was filled with the liquidy song of drowsy birds. Alexa experienced the sharp delight of the moment with a raw sensitivity that bordered on pain. She laid her cheek against the window frame, suddenly intensely glad to be alive and to be aware of the world around with such vividness, such profundity.

The next morning she telephoned Royston as soon as she got to work. 'I'm afraid he's in a meeting Miss Lockton,' his secretary explained politely. 'He won't be available until lunch-time. Can I give him a message?'

'No, no message, just tell him I called will you?' She replaced the receiver slowly, conscious that her future husband might not be an easy man to reach in a crisis. But then she was not in a crisis — was she?

The phone rang immediately. Hop

was not in yet to answer. Alexa spoke into it automatically. 'Good morning, Lockton's of Arkenfield.'

Frantic pips sounded on the line, then a click, then the purr of the dialling tone. A call from a phone box. They often caused problems. Hope appeared, twenty minutes late and full of apologies. 'Wretched kids', she said with affectionate irritation. 'Kate over-slept, then she couldn't find her Maths homework. Poor lamb, she was so upset I hadn't the heart to leave until we'd found it.' Kate was Hope's teenage daughter who relied heavily on her mother since her parents' divorce.

'Where was it?' Alexa asked, amused and sympathetic.

'In her school bag! She never thought to look there: too obvious!' Hope was suddenly serious. 'I'm really sorry, Alexa. It's rotten to be late when we're so busy.'

'Don't worry. You've worked late often enough. Kids are important as well as work.'

'Heavens — I'm glad I work for a woman. Men don't understand these things. I know. I've worked for some real rotters. Right then, I'll get on,' she said in her brisk Yorkshire fashion. 'Shall I bring you a coffee?'

'Yes, that would be lovely,' Alexa murmured.

Hope peered curiously at her. 'Are you O.K., Alexa? You look a bit washed out.'

'I'm fine. I just didn't sleep well, that's all.'

'You shouldn't take the business to bed with you,' Hope chuckled. 'There are much more interesting companions to be had!'

Recalling the thoughts she *had* taken to bed with her brought a gentle pinkness to Alexa's cheeks.

Hope said casually, 'Where's Rick? He's usually around long before I get here.'

'I don't know,' Alexa said slowly, 'he hasn't come in yet.' Her heart pounded heavily at the thought that Rick might have vanished as suddenly and inexplicably as he had come. Or perhaps he was ill, or had had an accident. The speculations whirled in her head, spiralling down into a pool of chronic anxiety.

'You're not fretting about him are you?' Hope grinned suggestively.

'No.' Alexa was firm. 'But I wish he'd hurry up. There's a lot of work to get through.'

'Mmn.' Hope munched her lip thoughtfully. 'Bit of a mystery our Rick isn't he? There's something about him I can't quite put my finger on!'

'I had the impression you would be very happy to put your finger on any part of him given the chance,' Alexa observed drily, recalling Hope's preference for beautiful young men.

'No, not Rick. He's out of my class.' Hope's eyes gleamed with wickedness. 'Hang it all — I am nearly forty you know!'

'I hadn't noticed that state being any handicap,' Alexa smiled. Hope maintained a steady stream of admirers, some of them considerably younger than herself.

'Perhaps not,' Hope said with a heavy stare, 'but as far as Rick is concerned I'm keeping my hands right off!'

'Really,' Alexa returned, as casually as she could manage.

'Oh yes, because you see, in my book, Rick — is yours!' With this bald announcement Hope departed to fetch the coffee, leaving Alexa with nerves shocked and jangling.

The time crawled on. Ten-thirty and still no Rick. Alexa initiated a customer into the delights of a dark blue Daimler Sovereign, thinking that cars were really expensive toys for adults, and all the time keeping half an eye on the street outside and willing a black-helmeted motor cyclist to appear.

'When can I take it for a test drive, love?' her customer asked, his cheerful, ruddy face full of admiration for the delicate, slender woman dressed rather severely in navy and white who was so obviously in command of herself and her small but growing empire.

She hesitated. 'I'd like to say you could take it right now — but I'm a little short-staffed at the moment.' She sized up the situation.

Three other cars needed to be moved before she could get the Daimler out of the showroom and she really didn't want to leave Hope alone with the telephone unrelentingly insistent and an accumulation of secretarial work. Oh Rick, Rick — where *are* you? 'Would this afternoon do?' she asked apologetically.

'Yes love, sure it will. The name's Sharp,' he told her, 'Sharp by name, and Sharp by nature. You won't take me for a ride you know!'

'I wouldn't presume to try, Mr Sharp,' she countered sweetly.

'No,' he nodded, 'you seem to be running a genuine outfit here. Bet you're making a tidy bit eh?'

Men! The cheek of them; the sheer, blatant nerve! 'I'm certainly not complaining,' she said diplomatically. She smiled politely as he left, then returned to her office and located the Daimler's documents; feeling pretty certain that Mr Sharp would clinch the deal without delay once he had driven the car.

She was vaguely aware of the outer door slamming and then of familiar footsteps hurtling up the stairs. Her relief was so great that her limbs quivered with excitation. But by the time Rick's large frame stood behind the desk, her anxiety and tumult of confused feelings had resolved themselves into one fierce emotion – anger. Like a loving mother who has been concerned for the well-being and safety of her child, all she could do was let rip at him. 'Where the hell have you been?' she demanded. 'It's nearly eleven!'

'I had some trouble with the bike,' he told her calmly, his eyes raking over her with a deep gaze, 'had to push it to the nearest garage.'

She frowned. 'Why didn't you telephone to let me know?'

'I did. Couldn't get through at the first call box and then the line was engaged all the time.'

She nodded, believing him.

'I'm really sorry, Alexa.' His low voice of apology sent ripples of longing through her stomach. 'I'll put in the extra time this evening.' He looked deep into her face. She knew that he was reliving those few incredible and wonderfully precious moments of the night before when they had been in each other's arms and nothing else in the world had mattered. He showed no trace of remorse, no regret, no hint of apology. She felt the colour wash up into her face in a great wave.

'It's all right,' she muttered, 'I'm sorry I snapped at you.'

'I'm flattered that you did. It suggests that you were worried about me,' he said softly.

'I'm worried about all the work that needs doing on my stock,' she retorted.

He grinned and made an exaggerated pretence of rolling up his sleeves.

'Don't be. I shall work at the speed of light.' The atmosphere was suddenly filled with his energy and vigour. Alexa had to admit to herself that she was inordinately pleased to see him. Vastly relieved also.

She smiled, wistful and bewildered.

'I told you I was going to make myself indispensable.' His eyes twinkled mischievously.

'You're impossible,' she murmured.

'No — just determined!' He moved to the door purposefully, then swung round and asked, 'Sleep well?'

She pursed her lips. 'As a matter of fact — no.'

'Good,' he said amiably, 'a hopeful sign.'

'Rick', she said sternly, 'I think . . . ' She could not think how to put it.

'Yes?' he smiled expectantly.

'About last night,' she told him firmly, 'I think I should explain . . . '

'Last night was beautiful,' he cut in with equal firmness. 'It needs no explanations.'

She tried to protest but he silenced her. 'Beautiful things speak for themselves Alexa, they need no futile words to explain them away!' He raised his eyebrows sardonically, blew her a kiss and was gone — taking the steps three at a time, humming to himself as he went.

Alexa closed her eyes momentarily. Hope buzzed through. 'Is that Superman I hear?' she queried.

'Who else?' Alexa said grimly.

'Great. I'll take him a coffee. I've got Mrs Wentworth on the line. Shall I put her through?'

A vision of Mrs Wentworth, Jaeger-suited, hair immaculately waved, Rayne court shoes gleaming swam into Alexa's mind's eye and inexplicably brought with it a tremor of guilt. She imagined Royston's impressively upright mother witnessing the passionate little scene in her showroom and felt prickles of sweat erupt in her armpits.

'Alexa dear! I'm *so* sorry to bother you at work.' Mrs Wentworth's voice radiated confidence.

I'll bet, Alexa thought wryly, judging that Mrs Wentworth would never dream of bothering her husband or Royston at work. She belonged to a breed and generation of women who would never be convinced that a woman's work could ever be as serious as a man's.

'Royston tells me that you've named the day at last!'

Alexa pressed her lips together. 'Yes — yes, I suppose so.'

'That's marvellous my dear. So exciting — a wedding in the family. We must get together to make plans,' she said conspiratorially. 'How about next Monday — so much better when the men aren't around to get under our feet. You can take an hour or two off can't you, dear, being your own boss?' Her tone was both cajoling and authoritative.

Alexa found herself agreeing almost automatically as though she had been run over by a velvet-covered steam roller. Mrs Wentworth's good-bye tinkled in her ear like a golden bell as she reflected how difficult she found it to be quietly assertive where personal relationships were concerned — yet never ever experienced that kind of difficulty with the customers. She really did not want to give up working time to have a little tête-à-tête with Mrs Wentworth; so why had she agreed to do so? She supposed that it was all part of the give and take required in family and married life.

Around lunch-time Rick bounded up the steps and presented himself unexpectedly in her room, a broad grin on his face and his arms filled with flowers — a fragrant, colourful riot of daffodils, irises, tulips and freesias all massed together in a lively, nodding bunch.

Alexa felt her mood lighten and her pulse speed up. 'What are those?' she asked, sucking in her cheeks and trying not to laugh.

'Flowers!' He inspected them with grave curiosity. 'Yes, quite definitely they're flowers.'

'Well?' she glanced up at him through her long lashes, knowing that her look was flirtatious and not being able to stop herself from thoroughly enjoying the deliciousness of the feeling.

'Blossoms for a wonderful, clever, sexy and totally adorable lady!'

'Go and give them to her then,' Alexa said coolly, aware that a flame of colour had rushed to her cheeks.

He laid them on the desk, fresh and dewy moist, their mingle of scents headily reminiscent of warm spring days when lovers would wander in the woods over carpets of bluebells with their arms wound around one another. 'No,' he said gently, 'I'd rather give them to you.' His eyes moved lingeringly over her face and body with provocative appraisal. The glance was as warm and deeply provocative as a frankly sexual caress.

'Rick!' she warned.

'O.K., O.K., I've made my point. I want you to understand about last night. You see I meant it — every word every kiss, every touch and I'm not going to let you forget it!'

As if I could she thought. 'Rick, I've got work to do,' she said briskly, '*You've* got work to do. I'd like you to get that Daimler out and give it a run round. There's a Mr Sharp coming at two o'clock . . . ,' her voice trailed off. Rick had leaned across the desk and laid a tender kiss on her neck.

'Rick! Stop it! DON'T!'

He gave her a long calm look.

'Rick!' she warned.

He placed his hand behind her neck, pulled her closer and kissed her again, his mouth caressing her cheek then moving to her lips, his tongue flicking over hers and sending a shower of fiery sparks darting through her body.

'Rick, for goodness' sake!'

'Yes, it's good isn't it? You and me kissing feels very good indeed. Why deny it?'

'My God, you're crazy. Have you ever heard of sexual harassment at work?'

He thought about it and winked at

her. 'Certainly have,' he said, 'and I'm not getting nearly enough!'

She burst into spontaneous laughter, picked up her desk calculator and took pretend aim.

'Hold it, I'm off!'

'I should think so!' She watched him through the window, shifting cars about, jumping in and out of them with energy, pushing one that stubbornly refused to start. Oh heavens, she thought, even the way he handles the *cars* is sexy.

She telephoned Royston. 'Darling — I've been trying to get you all morning!' she chided softly.

'Sorry,' he returned seriously, 'I've been really tied up.'

'Oh dear,' she sympathised. 'Look dear, come over to the flat tonight. I'll cook you something very special and we'll . . . we'll have a nice quiet time together.' It was as near to an invitation to seduction as she could get with Royston.

He cleared his throat noisily. 'That

sounds super but I'm flying out to Amsterdam this afternoon. There's a survey to do for one of our big Dutch clients.'

'Oh no! How long will you be away?'

'Just a couple of nights.'

A dark panic seized her. It was as though Royston were deserting her and leaving her exposed and undefended. She looked out at the blond hunk of manhood disappearing into the driving seat of the Daimler and wondered how much more of his persistent and passionate battering she could take without toppling off her carefully defended, chaste pedestal into a wild, crazy, inexorable whirlpool of desire and surrender.

'Alexa, are you still there?'

'Yes.'

'I'll be back for Friday — your birthday.'

'Oh yes.' She tried to pull herself back to normality.

'You haven't forgotten have you?' he joked. 'I've booked a table for two at

Grensham Hall, asked them to have the champagne on ice.'

'Oh good,' she said faintly, 'that will be lovely.'

'I hope you contacted that dressmaker of yours — about a very special dress,' he told her sternly.

'Oh yes, yes of course,' she said hurriedly, making a note in her diary, WEDDING DRESS, and underlining it three times.

At three o'clock a contented-looking Mr Sharp signed up to buy the Daimler and Alexa reflected that she was rapidly on her way to being in that enviable position when she would have to seriously consider the best ways of using all the money she was making. But despite these cheering thoughts the exertion and excitement of the past twenty-four hours was catching up with her. She rested her head on her hand and closed her eyes. Rick came in softly and hung some sets of keys on the board of hooks opposite her desk. 'You're worn out,' he commented, glancing at the droop of her shoulders.

'Yes,' she admitted, remarking to herself, not for the first time, on his sensitivity to the feelings of others; a quality she found rare in most men. 'I am tired.'

'Call it a day,' he said abruptly.

'No, I can't leave now!'

'Yes you can. Hope and I can manage. You've no more appointments have you?'

'Well . . . no.'

He took her black three-quarter length jacket from its hanger and held it out for her as waiters do in the best restaurants.

'You're bullying me Rick,' she smiled, rather enjoying it, and deciding that this idea was a good one after all.

'Take a break,' he murmured, sliding the coat gently over her shoulders and touching her neck lightly. She shivered with the electric excitement of his closeness. 'Do what other women do for a change.'

'And what is that?' she demanded,

turning to face him with a mischievous, questioning look.

'Oh — curl up with a book, have her hair done, browse round the shops, drink a glass of wine . . . make love!'

Alexa pinkened. 'Yes, well, I'm sure I'll find something suitable to occupy myself with.'

'I sincerely hope it is some*thing*,' he drawled. 'I'd hate to think it was some*one* — when the worthy Royston is working his socks off and your poor lowly henchman,' he tugged at a lock of unruly hair, 'is up to his armpits in grease!'

'You have an insatiable appetite for sexual innuendo,' she told him tartly. 'If you're feeling frustrated Rick, I suggest you go out and find a nice cuddly girl-friend to keep you company. Do what other men do for a change,' she concluded with sharp challenge.

'*Touché*,' he grinned, unabashed. 'Perhaps I'll take your advice.'

Recalling those last words as she settled herself in the Jaguar, Alexa felt something unpleasantly akin to jealousy. Imagining Rick with some adoring girl on his knee, laughing into his blue eyes and nibbling at his ear was not a happy prospect. She put her foot down on the accelerator with needless ferocity and overtook a surprised looking young mother driving a Mini Metro bursting with squabbling school children. She wondered what to do. Suddenly she remembered that she had not contacted the dressmaker. Damn. It occurred to her that she could simply drop in on her dressmaker; kill two birds with one stone, start making plans for the important dress and have a delicious browse through all those fascinating fabrics and patterns. Sarah Nichols and her husband were struggling to get their design and couture business off the ground. They each had part-time jobs, but one of them was always available in the studio they had created in the attic of their small town house. Sarah made all Alexa's formal business suits and probably knew the intimate details of her slender figure better than anyone else. 'Hello Miss Lockton — come up!' Sarah went clumping ahead of Alexa in her squashy flat-heeled boots and her swirling skirt. Around her neck was a decoration which looked as though it had been assembled from recycled golf balls. She had a style and flamboyance which Alexa found totally appealing. 'Here's some super material that would make up into a lovely jacket for you,' Sarah said, throwing a bolt of cloth onto the long cutting table and letting the soft sheen of alpaca and mohair flow over it in cobalt blue ripples.

Alexa regarded the fabric with interest.

'Yes, that's very nice — but I'm wanting a dress — a wedding dress,' she said briskly, alarmed at the strange sensation of sinking that was going on in her stomach.

'Oh, marvellous!' Sarah looked at her client tactfully. Wedding dresses were always emotional projects, required very gentle handling. She got out sketches, swatches of fabric, sat Alexa down and poured her a sherry.

'Something simple I think,' Alexa mused, mindful of Royston's rather conservative tastes.

Eventually they narrowed the field down to cream silk in a Tudor style with a stiff stand-up collar. Sarah replenished the sherry glasses. 'Celebration,' she smiled.

They sipped together in quiet reflection. Alexa looked around the walls where garments in varying stages of development hung, partly covered in tissue paper. Vivid pinks and greens rested side by side with sober greys and navies; frills and ruffles contrasted with the classical tailoring of neat lapels. Sarah's room was a place of magic — a Santa Claus's grotto for grown-ups.

'Mmn, I like that,' Alexa murmured, eyeing a full skirt of palest peach silk caught up to reveal a tantalising glimpse of frilled petticoat the shade of Cornish butter.

Sarah jumped up and whipped off the tissue to disclose a buttery-coloured blouse, light and gauzy, cut wide across the neck with elaborately puffed sleeves and a shamefully voluptuous trimming of lace.

'They're beautiful,' Alexa exclaimed, although she normally preferred more classically cut clothes.

'The disaster of the month,' Sarah grinned wryly. 'The customer gave me a free hand and then hated the results; wouldn't buy them.'

'Oh, they're for sale then. I'll slip them on!'

Sarah plucked at the sleeves of the blouse, arranging the folds to hang gracefully over Alexa's wrists. 'How strange. I could have made it just for you. Perfect!'

Alexa wrote a cheque on the spot and watched as Sarah laid the garments tenderly in an ocean of tissue paper and eased them into the distinctive gold and pink bags with her name on.

Whenever shall I wear these, Alexa

wondered, smiling at Sarah and enjoying the sensation of buying something completely impractical just for once.

⋆ ⋆ ⋆

The next morning Alexa returned to work refreshed and full of energy. She had decided, for her own peace of mind, that it would be wise to arrange things so that she and Rick were not thrown together during the next few days and she fixed up a number of appointments which involved him in delivering cars to customers who lived some distance away. Rick had proved himself unfailingly reliable in his relationships with customers and she had every confidence in his ability to deal with any of the little problems and complaints which inevitably cropped up in everyday contact with them.

She had an obscure conviction that if she could somehow avoid any kind of clash or emotional confrontation with Rick until Royston returned, she would remain safe. By standing firmly on dry ground she would be in no danger of being swept away on a great tidal wave of sensation. And once Royston was back she intended to occupy herself with him to the exclusion of any other man.

Two days later when Hope brought her afternoon cup of coffee she also delivered an unexpected admonishment. 'Alexa, I'm sorry to sound critical, but there's something I have to say to you.'

'Mmn,' Alexa was deep in the preparation of an invoice.

'It's about Rick. You're working him too hard. He wouldn't dream of telling you so I'm doing it instead.'

Alexa looked up startled. 'What on earth are you talking about?'

'Rick's been out seeing customers nearly all the time for the past couple of days and he's still keeping up with all the cleaning and maintenance work.' Hope spoke with stern patience.

Alexa frowned. She prided herself on

keeping a keen eye on the welfare of her staff but she realised now that she had been so preoccupied with keeping Rick at arm's length that she had quite omitted to consider his work-load and well-being. Hope was quite right. He had taken on all the extra commitments she had given him, without a word of complaint, and had still managed to ensure that every vehicle in the place was immaculate — ready for the most searching inspection at any time.

'When is he doing the preparation work?' she asked slowly.

'At night,' Hope said flatly, 'very late.'

'How do you know?'

'I was out at a party last night. On the way home I came past here, saw Rick in the showroom working on the black Alfa Romeo.'

'What time was that?'

'Eleven-thirty, midnight maybe.'

'Oh heavens!'

Hope looked at her curiously. 'It's not like you Alexa, being so unaware of what's going on'.

'No.'

'Is there a problem between you and Rick?' Hope asked gently. 'I'm not going to pry — but if you need a sympathetic ear — you know where to find one.'

Alexa smiled gratefully at her departing back. She wondered how much Hope guessed. Quite a lot probably. She was a shrewd assessor of human beings and their frailties — yet never judgemental or prone to gossip. No wonder there was always a guy in tow. Men went for other qualities than a nice figure and a pretty face, whatever the glossy magazines maintained.

Alexa called Rick into her office when he returned that evening. 'Sit down Rick,' she said, assuming a quiet command that came very easily now that their conversation was to be on business terms. She saw immediately how tired he was. The big frame still hummed with energy, but the bright, merry blue eyes had dark rings underneath — a sure sign of fatigue.

Physical exertion was exhausting. Alexa knew that. When she first started her business she had done everything herself. Washed and polished the cars at the back of the premises, then stripped off her overalls and dashed around to the showroom in her one and only correct suit to deal with customers. Things were very different now, but she had not forgotten the crushing weariness brought about by hard manual work.

He looked at her quizzically. Fighting off her impulse to take his head in her arms, cradle him against her breast and stroke that wonderful lion's mane of hair, she said in clinical tones, 'I owe you an apology.'

He gave a puzzled frown. 'No,' his voice was husky, 'you've nothing to be sorry for as regards me.'

'I've been blind to the fact that you've had too much work to do.'

Rick frowned, spread out his hands thoughtfully and allowed her to proceed without making any comment.

'Hope saw you last night, very late, working on the Alfa.'

'Caught out!' he grinned. 'Have I been a bad boy? Do I get a smack?'

She refused to treat the matter lightly. 'Has it happened before?'

'No — well not as late as that,' he said significantly.

'Rick, you should have told me. And why haven't you been claiming overtime?'

'I suppose I just haven't got round to it yet. You see Alexa, apart from the fact that as a woman you're the most desirable in the world — as a boss you have a knack of inspiring terrific loyalty. We'd all work our guts out for you — overtime or not!'

She took a deep, shuddering breath. 'Thanks,' she said briskly, 'but I won't continue to inspire loyalty will I, if I'm so chronically unaware of one of my employee's determined efforts to work himself into the ground.'

'There's only one reason why a woman as good at her job as you would be chronically unaware,' Rick commented, having attended carefully to her little speech.

'Oh.' She swallowed down the lump that had lodged in her throat.

'Just one reason why she should be affected by temporary blindness.' He sliced a mocking glance at her.

She raised her chin in challenge. 'Don't go on,' she whispered savagely, 'I know what you're going to say — and it's not true!'

'Oh yes, you're blind all right, Alexa. Blind to the fact that there's more going between the two of us after a few short weeks than there will ever be in a lifetime between you and Royston Wentworth.'

'No — no, no, no!' She thumped her fist on the desk.

He grinned. 'Methinks the lady doth protest too much,' he murmured.

'Oh heavens, you're totally outrageous and impossible. How can I take you seriously?' she snapped.

'It's time you stopped being so

serious, Alexa. Grab life by the throat for a change. Have fun. Live dangerously.' He smiled roguishly down at her whilst her heart played tunes on her ribs. 'And don't worry about me,' he added with a grin, 'it'll be a long time before I'm six feet under. I've a whole lot of living and loving to do first.' He stared meaningfully at her.

'I think you should take the day off tomorrow,' she protested faintly. 'Take a break.' Give me a break, she added to herself.

'No chance!' he told her firmly. 'I'm taking a car to show our friend Armitage — don't you remember? I wouldn't miss that for the world.'

She laughed. 'Yes, I can see that I mustn't deprive you of that little treat. O.K. then, you win. Business as usual tomorrow. But no more slaving away at midnight. I shall keep a close eye on you.'

'I can't imagine a more beautiful eye to be under than yours,' he told her.

'Get out Rick,' she said with quiet

menace, 'before I do something I'd regret.'

He jumped up and blew her a kiss. 'Promises, promises,' he murmured. 'If only I could believe that one day you really would do something wonderfully wicked enough to regret.' He narrowed his eyes playfully, 'but only with me, of course. Don't you dare be wicked with anyone else!'

* * *

On her birthday Alexa decided to dispense with her usual sober greys and navies and blacks and put on a dress of coral pink, belted tightly at the waist with a stiffened cummerbund on which a bold *diamanté* butterfly perched.

As she drove into work the chill of the early May morning pierced through the silver sunshine and there was a light sieving of frost sprinkled underneath the hedges and glinting from tiny crevices in the drystone walls which snaked across the Yorkshire fields. She thought of Royston in Amsterdam and pictured the vast Dutch landscape splodged with the brilliant colour of thousand upon thousand of tulips. She and Royston must take some time off and go and see them together. Perhaps next spring. They were both so heavily committed, not doing nearly enough together at the moment.

Rick had already left to demonstrate a choice XJ6 to Mr Armitage when Alexa arrived behind her desk. She had not dared risk letting him know it was her birthday. Goodness knows what lengths he might go to. She recalled the flowers he had given her, still headily fragrant and fresh, forming a brilliant wedge of colour on the polished oak desk in her sitting-room. He had left a little note letting her know that he would be back mid morning. She looked thoughtfully at the writing; bold, decisive and stylish — that of an educated man with a mind of his own. Hope was quite right. There were quite a number of little puzzles surrounding

Rick. But he was doing work. She was inclined to let sleeping dogs lie.

'Hey — lover boy is here!' Hope announced brightly, appearing in the doorway with the inevitable coffee and glancing out through the window behind Alexa's chestnut head. Instantly Rick's rakish smile and sharp, twinkling eyes came swerving into Alexa's mind. Her heart hit against her ribs. She turned and watched as a navy blue BMW glided to a halt outside and her navy pin-stripe clad fiancé stepped out. A flush of horrified shame burned in her cheeks at the realisation that she could think of anyone but Royston in connection with the term 'lover' — let alone Rick Markland. For God's sake, she told herself irritably, pull yourself together.

She put her arms around Royston's neck and kissed the freshly shaved skin which had that expensively clean smell that well established men can afford. 'Darling,' she murmured, 'it's lovely to see you!' She wanted him to kiss her, sweep her into his arms and stamp out Rick Markland's insistent image which seemed permanently lodged behind her eyelids.

He kissed her politely, then reached into his pocket for a small box. 'Happy birthday,' he said. His face looked creased with anxiety. Business worries must be pressing on him, Alexa thought. The furrows along his forehead seemed to deepen every time she saw him. Poor Royston. He needed a break.

'Sit down,' she told him gently.

'No, no, I really mustn't stay.' He seemed agitated, poised for flight. The box contained pearl earrings; tiny, delicate, genuine pearls set in platinum. They would have cost a fortune. Alexa's mouth trembled in a smile of gratitude mingled with a strange disappointment that Royston could have made such a spectacular mistake. Had he not noticed her taste for the dramatic in her jewellery, her liking to make a strong statement with big shiny studs or Victorian pendants garnished with peridots or amethyst or citrine? The pearls were exquisite — but so safely discreet — exactly what his mother would choose to wear. In fact she recalled Mrs Wentworth's wearing some very similar.

A band of ice clutched around her chest as she digested this thought. 'They're beautiful,' she said firmly, 'but you've been far too generous!'

'You're my future wife,' he said matter-of-factly, 'you deserve the very best.'

Alexa turned away briefly. 'What time will you pick me up tonight? I'm really looking forward to it.' Her tone was bright and brittle.

There was a pause. 'I'll need to check, let you know this afternoon.'

'Is anything wrong?' she asked. 'Did the Amsterdam trip go well?'

'Fine. Bernard Horst flew back with me. We might be opening a big new account with his group.'

'Oh — how exciting!' The idea of new business, of any sort, sent the adrenalin racing in Alexa's veins.

'Mmn, I got the feeling he was wanting to fix up a dinner tonight for all the senior directors to firm up the plans . . . '

'Oh, but Royston!'

'Yes, yes darling I know. It's your birthday and we're going out. No problem. I'll put him off. Don't worry.'

Alexa looked at him with troubled eyes. She could tell that he was in some conflict about this proposed arrangement, which was obviously very important. It was her usual practice to be unfailingly accommodating about any of his business commitments. She took them very seriously as she would expect him to take hers. But tonight was different. It was her birthday — a time when she should take preference over everyone.

A Jaguar pulled up behind Royston's BMW. Alexa's eyes were drawn to Rick's energetic figure as he swung himself from the driving seat, slammed the door and bounded into the showroom. Her heart began to pound with sickening intensity.

Completing his usual frantic hurtle up the stairs, Rick burst into her office, giving only a cursory knock. 'Cracked it,' he exclaimed, tossing a bunch of keys onto her desk, 'clinched the deal just like that!' His blue eyes shone with wicked excitement.

Alexa knew the thrill of making a big sale. She tuned in with his mood instantly, smiling up at Rick and sharing his delight.

'Oh — I'm sorry to butt in,' Rick said with genuine contrition, realising that she was not alone.

Royston was presenting a distinctly chilly aspect. The two men's glances locked together with all the friendliness of a reindeer's antlers.

'Hullo, Mr Wentworth,' Rick said calmly, 'I do apologise, I got a little carried away with my success. I'll disappear. Plenty of work to be done!' Turning his back on Royston, Rick gave himself licence to close one eyelid in an unhurried and shamelessly intimate wink. Alexa felt like a schoolgirl trying not to laugh in Assembly.

'Have you put that fellow onto sales now?' Royston asked with tight annoyance as Rick departed. He had never trusted the handsome blond with the rippling muscles who, irritatingly enough, seemed to have an insatiable capacity for work.

'He's more than capable,' Alexa said evenly, 'and I'm very pushed at present to handle all the incoming business myself.'

'Huh, I'm surprised you let him go and see customers looking like that; he needs a good wash and a haircut.'

She bit her lip in silence.

'Look Alexa, I must dash. I'll call you this afternoon.'

But he did not call in the afternoon; it was seven when the phone eventually rang. Alexa had returned to her flat an hour before, had showered, then dowsed herself in Diorella — talc, body lotion, eau-de-toilette. She had dressed in blue satin underwear — a silky teddy and filmy stockings. Over the top went a slim-fitting black dress which clung softly to her small, slender frame. She fingered the pearl earrings thoughtfully, then slipped them onto her ears.

A bottle of her very favourite 1979 Vouvray went into the frig, and she prepared some delicate, piquant canapés of smoked salmon and asparagus. She and Royston would have a quiet aperitif together before they went out.

She wished he would call soon and almost ran to the phone when it commenced its warble.

'Alexa — look I'm really sorry but I'm afraid we'll have to change our plans for this evening.' Royston set out on a long explanation; something about Bernard Horst and the Amsterdam account and an urgent business dinner.

Alexa listened uncomprehendingly. 'But it's my birthday,' she protested like a disappointed child.

'Darling — I know. I'll come on later, as soon as I can,' he said soothingly,

'We'll go out tomorrow instead.'

'But Royston, it's my birthday today and I want you *now*!' Tears of rage and frustration pricked behind her eyelids.

There was an intense silence down the phone, then Royston's voice began murmuring apologies again. He sounded so calm. He was not in touch with her feelings at all.

She drew in a deep breath. 'All right, Royston. I take your point. Let's just leave it that I'll see you tomorrow night.'

'But what about later this evening?' he queried anxiously.

'Forget that darling, don't give it another thought,' she said sweetly, replacing the handset carefully and cutting him off. He would ring back of course. She stared defiantly at the phone. It was silent. She went through to the kitchen for a glass of wine. It would be sure to ring then; phones always did the minute you left them. She uncorked the Vouvray. The phone warbled fruitily. She sucked in her cheeks and smiled. Eyes narrowed slightly she approached the instrument with calm deliberation. 'Hullo,' she said, her voice warm but firm.

'Alexa?'

'Yes?' This wasn't Royston she thought in confusion. Her heart speeded up in swift realisation.

'It's Rick. I'm sorry to bother you at home.'

'That's all right. What is it, Rick?'

'The keys for Armitage's Jag — I need them to lock it up.'

'Yes?'

'Have you got them?'

She frowned. She opened her bag. 'Oh heavens, I must have scooped them up off the desk by mistake. How stupid of me?'

'Easily done,' he said cheerily. 'I'll pop along and get them.'

'Oh no, I'll bring them down. I'm not doing . . . ' she bit her lip.

He caught her discomfiture. 'Are you O.K., Alexa?

'Yes, of course.'

'Sit tight then. It's no trouble. It's a special night for you, Hope told me. You'll be getting ready for Prince Charming. You can toss the keys down to me in the car park — like a fairy princess flinging pennies to the poor. I'll tug at my forelock and retire gracefully.'

Alexa moistened her lips, a dizzy recklessness washing over her in a delicious flood. 'You'll do no such thing Rick. You'll come to the front door and you'll come in and have a birthday drink.' Her voice was deep and soft with invitation.

There was a short silence, then a long, low whistle from Rick.

'Don't go away,' he instructed, 'I'll be right there!'

The phone clicked. Alexa stared at it. 'Oh God,' she groaned, 'what on earth have I done?'

4

Alexa poured herself a glass of Vouvray. Its coolness glazed the long-stemmed glass with a mist of teardrops. She arranged the canapés on a boat-shaped copper dish and put them on the heavy glass-topped table by the fireplace. Standing at the window she chewed her finger nervously and glanced out into the garden. The lawn, close-clipped after the first cutting of summer, meandered away into a little wood at the back of the house where a mass of bluebells slumbered in the pinkish dusk. A wood pigeon skimmed over the length of the grass, one wing uptilted giving it the appearance of a racing yacht. The sky, glowing sharply blue at its apex was furled with white wisps of cloud forming a pattern as regular as herringbone tweed. She sighed, her breath thickened and jerky.

She heard the very first low throbbings of the motor cycle with a shiver of apprehension. Rick was waving enthusiastically the minute he turned in at the gates, ringing the doorbell in seconds, all energy and high spirits as usual.

She opened the door and his blinding blue gaze locked into hers with electric force. 'Hullo,' she said faintly, feeling naked and undefended meeting him outside the protecting confines of the business.

'Happy birthday,' he smiled. 'I thought you were going to invite me in,' he added playfully, pushing gently past her and closing the door.

She swallowed, sensing a constraint in her voice as she invited him to sit down, then poured him some wine.

'Cheers,' he said, raising his glass. 'I wish I'd known it was your birthday; I'd have filled with your arms with roses — you lovely lady!'

'Oh Rick, you say the most outrageously flattering things,' she smiled.

'I tell the truth,' he grinned, 'if that

happens to be flattering, so much the better. Why keep the nice thoughts in?'

His direct candour relaxed her immediately. She sniffed at the pale glistening wine and felt the irritation of the last few hours dissolved away.

'I brought you this,' he said, reaching into the inner pocket of his anorak, 'I got it when I was taking 'O' levels — it's always been rather special to me. Will you have it please?'

Alexa reached across and took the slim leather book gently from his hands. It was a volume of Shakespeare's sonnets. Inside was inscribed, 'R.Markland' in boyish writing. She was so touched that tears sprang to her eyes. 'Yes, I'd love to have it.' She brushed his fingers lightly, feeling once again the powerful connection between them and noticing with a blend of gratefulness and regret that Rick was behaving impeccably. He had in no way used the situation to press any advances on her.

He regarded her thoughtfully, then drained his glass. 'Well — I suppose I'd better push off. Mustn't queer the pitch for Prince Charming — not on your special night. Even *I* have more tact than that!' He levered his big frame from her Victorian gentleman's chair and smiled down at her. He wore just a simple blue T-shirt under his anorak and Alexa could see the lines of his chest quite clearly. At his throat a pulse throbbed rhythmically.

She wanted to stand up on tiptoe and press her lips on that warm beat of life, fold herself close against him, fuse and merge with him and erase all the space between them. Oh God!

'Is something wrong?' he asked huskily — perceptive as usual.

'Royston can't make it!' she said baldly.

Rick stared in astonishment. 'Can't make it!' he rapped out. 'Is he ill?'

Alexa turned troubled eyes up to him and shook her head slowly. 'A business engagement.'

'The bastard,' Rick said venomously. 'I'll kick his teeth in.'

'I don't think that would be very helpful,' she murmured with a rueful smile.

They stared at each other solemnly, each having the same thought and a perfect awareness that it was a shared one.

'Well,' he said cheerily, 'there's nothing for it but for me to act as stand in.'

'Why not?' Alexa said, full of mischief. What the hell! Royston had let her down. Why should she consider the niceties of his feelings?

'He seems to have done me a good turn,' Rick smiled, 'perhaps I'll leave his teeth intact after all. Where shall we go then?'

'I don't know. We were going to Grensham Hall . . . '

'Uh-huh — classy tastes. You need to take out a mortgage before going there. I don't think I'm quite up to that tonight!'

'Oh Rick — I'm not letting you pay,' she said sternly.

'Oh yes you are. This is going to be my treat. I'm an old-fashioned guy — give a lady flowers, feed her chocolates, pay the bills — act like boss in bed!'

She swallowed hard. 'Well in that case I think we'd better go halves.'

'Nonsense. I'll be the perfect gent. Pay the bill and let you off with a chaste good-night kiss at the door.'

Even the thought of that little crumb of passion sent Alexa's blood on some frantic journey around her veins. She wondered if she had made a desperate mistake. She had invited Rick round for a drink in the sure knowledge that they would wind up spending the evening together. And to spend an evening with Rick, given her crazy yearning for his wonderful, tough male body was sheer madness; like walking on the edge of a cliff knowing that she could topple over and fall and fall clutching at black emptiness. But somehow, deep in her heart, she knew that it was right for her to be with Rick. In some obscure way they fitted together, for all their differences of social and financial status they matched each other. She did not understand it. She only knew that the pleasure of being in his company was more fierce and relentless than anything she had known before.

'I'll take you on a mystery tour,' he decided, 'on the bike. Would you like that?'

Her eyes sparkled gleefully. 'Yes — oh yes!'

'You look a little formal,' he ventured, eyeing the classically cut black crêpe and adding darkly, 'for what I had in mind.'

'I'll change,' she said. 'Pour yourself more wine Sir Galahad and make yourself at home as the saying goes.'

She pressed a recording of Handel's 'Water Music' into the tape deck, knowing that he liked the baroque era of music. Resisting the impulse to ruffle the thick blond hair playfully as she passed his chair, she went swiftly into her bedroom, slid back the wardrobe door and pursed her lips in thought. The new peach skirt and the cream blouse caught her eye instantly. Here was the perfect opportunity to wear them. She slipped them on and chose flattish cream leather pumps to balance their frothy fullness. She replaced the pearl earrings with big gypsy-type hoops of gold, fluffed her hair out and sprayed on more Diorella — feeling dreamy and soft and feminine.

Rick was squatting down peering curiously at her collection of books and tapes. He swivelled round to look at her, his eyes travelling from her head to her toes in a leisurely and gently devouring fashion. 'Beautiful,' he murmured hoarsely. He sprang up and came towards her, seizing both hands and opening her arms wide. 'You look like a shepherdess,' he teased, 'a Dresden China shepherdess, delicate and exquisite — and oh so fragile!'

'Fragile! A shepherdess!' she laughed. 'You're like Hope — a true romantic.'

'Yes I am,' he agreed undismayed.

'Come live with me and be my love, you beautiful shepherdess,' he quoted.

'That's poetry, written years ago — an old line!' she chided.

His eyes sharpened with interest at her recognition. 'Never mind if Christopher Marlowe said it first — I'm saying it now,' he told her. 'Come away with me this instant,' he persisted provocatively, 'come live with me and be my love — for ever!'

She wriggled out of his reach in alarm as he moved towards her. 'Rick, don't make things difficult.'

'I'm simply declaring love on you. What's the problem?' He paused. 'Ah yes. The problem, as I remember, is attending a business dinner on your special day. The problem is, in short, an unfeeling, undeserving bas . . . '

'Don't say it,' she cried in distress, 'I'm going to marry him!'

His blue eyes blazed into hers — dark, brilliant blue, flecked with gold like a tiger. Handel's triumphant chords drummed in their ears as the seconds passed. 'Rick, will you promise not to say anything about Royston for the rest of the evening. Promise or I won't come,' she said in agitation.

'O.K. I promise.' His eyes carried a look of resignation.

He made her put on a warm jacket against the chill felt on the bike, even in early summer. She tucked her hair inside the spare helmet he kept in the carrier, vaulted lightly on to the pillion seat and wrapped her arms around him firmly. Revelling in the hardness of his strong body between her arms she hugged him fiercely. 'Oh God,' she told him, 'as I've gone completely mad I might as well enjoy myself!'

'That's the spirit,' he agreed, seizing a hand and crushing a passionate kiss onto it. 'Spontaneity is a delightful and much neglected aspect of human behaviour.'

Alexa felt the urgent throb of the motor between her thighs. Rick drove safely as usual, observing speed limits in the town, but once out in the country accelerating so that they seemed to fly, sending hedges and fields and grazing cattle reeling and spinning into the distance. She had no idea where they were going, she simply abandoned herself to sensation, the noise, the wind, the speed of cutting through the clean air, the feeling of being completely united with the firm warmth of Rick's body.

He took her to a small market town some miles north of Arkenfield and parked in the stone cobbled square guarded by an old market cross with a quaint weather-beaten clock at its summit. 'Did you know that the town crier still heralds dusk and dawn here?' he asked her as they shook their hair free of the helmets and rubbed their ears to restore normal hearing.

'Yes,' she said sweetly. 'I do have some knowledge outside trade-in prices and gear ratios, you may be surprised to learn!'

'Sorry I spoke,' he grinned aiming a playful punch at her nose.

They descended stone steps into a cellar where laughing couples and groups sat drinking wine and eating delicious smelling food. Rick settled her at a table and handed her a wine list of commendable length and variety. 'Red or white?' he asked.

She shrugged. What did it matter?

He ordered a bottle of each and they sat smiling at each other over the tiny table, bare except for their glasses and a wavering candle placed in an empty champagne bottle over whose neck the grease of dozens of similar candles had wept thickly. They chose chicken in garlic and a green salad and waited in anticipation.

'Tell me!' he said in a low voice.

'Tell you what?'

'Everything. I want to know everything about you, you beautiful, wanton shepherdess — and don't think I didn't notice those hugs and squeezes on the bike!'

'Rick!' she warned.

'We're not at work now. I can allow

myself a free rein.'

'I haven't noticed you ever doing anything else.' She took a roguish sip of wine.

'Come on,' he urged, 'what about the life history. I'm hungry for information. Hungry for everything else too!' he added wickedly.

'Well what you'll get is short and to the point. I hate to disappoint you but I had a very happy and uneventful childhood. My parents live in a little bungalow in Derbyshire, my brother goes to medical school, my father is a maths teacher and my mother does part-time nursing. They have a comfortable but modest existence — and so did I as a child. End of story!'

'So why aren't you a teacher, a nurse or a budding doctor?'

She smiled. 'Everything was so safe, so secure. I wanted to break out, take risks, fly a little.'

'That's wonderful!' His eyes shone with anticipation.

'Before you get carried away,' she

interposed drily, 'I should add that I also wanted to make money. I wanted to have beautiful things, not always have to be careful and sensible and make do with second best.' She looked down at the supple kid leather pumps; lovely shoes had been one of her especial weaknesses since the business started to yield a healthy profit. 'Simple, ordinary greed Rick — just like ninety-nine per cent of the rest of the population.'

'You're not greedy. You wear marvellous clothes — but you haven't got all that many, you drive a second-hand car and your flat is filled with things which are unusual rather than expensive.' His level gaze challenged her tenderly.

'Anything else to report Hawk-Eye?' she teased, deeply impressed by the extent and accuracy of his observation.

'Just that ninety-nine per cent of the population don't actually get out there and do anything about their greedy desires.'

'So I get ten out of ten for effort?' she

remarked wryly.

'Yes.' He narrowed his eyes. 'And stop sending yourself up. I take you very seriously. You have a phenomenal capacity for work. I've never known a woman like you.'

'But plenty of men probably,' she retorted, automatically on the defensive. Her experience had taught her to be very wary of male flattery as regards her business success. It often concealed derision and a deep-seated desire to push her firmly back into her woman's place. And what would Rick understand of that. He was a man, for goodness' sake. 'Alexa,' he told her warningly. 'plenty of guys might try to put you down on the work score. But not me. Give me credit at least for a genuine admiration of professionalism — even if you give me credit for nothing else.'

She reached out for his hand impulsively and pressed it to her cheek. 'I'm sorry,' she whispered, 'but don't get the idea that I'm perfect. That's too much to live up to.'

'You're certainly not perfect,' he drawled, 'you're quite capable of making the most elementary and horrendous errors of judgement. One at any rate.'

She stared at him, absorbing the implication behind his words. The grey upright image of Royston Wentworth rose up between them as guilt inducing as Marley's ghost. 'Don't,' she whispered, 'don't, you promised!'

'Yes, O.K. I did.' He poured her more wine and began to question her closely on the details of setting up the business. He listened fascinated as she told him of her battle with her parents to leave school early and turn down a university career, of the experience she gained with a car hire firm, of her capitalising on the unexpected legacy from a distant aunt in order to start up on her own.

'This is becoming very one-sided. I'm not talking about myself any more,' she said firmly after a while. 'What about you Rick. I hardly know anything. I don't even know where you live.'

'I rent the ground floor of a tiny cottage just outside Arkenfield. You can come and see it on the way back.' He winked invitingly.

'Oh no, I don't think so,' she replied hastily, scenes of intimacy leaping to mind with disturbing temptation.

He sighed. 'Have some more wine,' he pleaded. 'It doesn't seem to be having the slightest effect on you. If I'd any ideas of getting you tight and having my evil way with you — I'd be a very disappointed man!'

She chuckled. 'You know,' she remarked with careful consideration, 'you haven't fooled me, Rick. I knew there was something different about you right from the first time we met.'

'Oh yes, go on.' He leaned forward with interest.

'That casual confidence in recommending yourself for the job, that little phrase '*à bientôt*' — so chic and French, the liking for baroque music, the knowledge of poetry.'

'Well,' he said with mocking menace, 'do continue.'

'And the way you speak. You're not a local man are you?'

'Almost. Not so far away at any rate.'

She was surprised. 'Really. You've no Yorkshire accent.'

'Neither have you. Neither has Prince Charming.'

'No — but . . . '

'But you'd expect a working man to speak 'all broad like'. Is that it?'

'Let's put it this way, Rick — all my other assistants have. I'm no snob,' she warned him, 'but I do notice things about people.'

'Who's the Hawk-Eye now?' he smiled. 'All right, you're forgiven. You're no snob. But don't put me in a pigeon hole. I am what I am and I haven't told you any lies and I'm a damned good worker — aren't I?'

'Yes,' she said quietly, 'you're quite exceptional.'

They talked and talked, looking deep

into each other's eyes — their hearts and minds completely at ease. The candle sank slowly down, swelling the neck of the bottle with warm, waxy teardrops. Alexa forgot the time. She wanted the evening to last and last like a child seeking to capture those precious moments at the end of a birthday and prevent them from dashing away into the past. The little cellar was almost empty. Girls in skin-tight jeans and dangling earrings came to clear the tables. Just one couple remained.

'You've got an admirer,' Rick grinned, sliding his eyes to the elegant grey-haired man watching Alexa with interest. She looked across and smiled, happy and flattered.

The night air hit them like a stinging slap. Rick put an arm protectively around her shoulders as they walked to the bike. 'I don't ever want to let you go,' he murmured, his breath warm against her ear.

'I know the feeling,' she whispered,

holding him tight as they sped through the velvet blackness of the night, the lights of the bike carving a cone of white brilliance ahead of them. She could feel her skirt billowing out like a spinnaker sail so that she was riding the wind, her spirit free to roam wherever it wished.

He walked with her to the door, leaning against the frame and regarding her sardonically as she placed her key in the lock with an amazingly steady hand. 'I've had an evening of magic,' he said.

'Yes, so have I.' She put her hand up to stroke his cheek. 'Thank you, Rick. Thank you so much. I'm very grateful.'

'Uh-huh. Do I turn into a white rat now,' he asked, 'like Cinderella's footman? Am I dismissed — just like that?'

'Rick, please,' she said, her eyes wide with fear at what further reckless behaviour she might indulge in if he did not leave immediately. Rick was working his way into her heart — and that meant he was trouble, big trouble. He had to go now, even though she wanted him to stay. More than anything she wanted him to stay.

'Invite me in Alexa,' he commanded in a low voice, 'please invite me in.'

'Oh God,' she cried in panic, 'all that flirting between us — it was just a joke — just fun. It didn't mean anything.' She was gabbling incoherently.

'Like hell it was a joke.' His eyes snapped with fire.

She was shocked. She had never heard him harsh and grating before. His easy-going, gay amiability had been temporarily replaced by an intensity, a savageness that seemed quite alien.

She trembled inwardly.

He gripped her shoulders, his fingers as tight as a vice. 'If that's what you call a joke, there's something seriously wrong with your sense of humour,' he growled softly.

He pushed the door open with his foot, reached down behind her knees and picked her up in his arms, carrying her through into the darkened hallway and closing the door firmly behind them.

* * *

After a long silence filled with the warmth of his lips and his soft probing tongue, Rick said, 'Now do you want me to go?'

'No,' she moaned, 'don't go. Don't ever go.'

He lifted her into his arms again and carried her through into the bedroom. Alexa felt the rest of the world spinning dizzily away into the distance so that her only world was with Rick, enclosed in his arms.

She expected him to lay her on the bed, to kiss her and take her clothes off — expected it, wanted it, would do nothing to prevent it. But instead he placed her on her feet, held her against him and began to rub the back of her neck with his big gentle hand. He found that tender spot that her grandfather would stroke when she was a child.

No-one else had ever touched her like that. She shuddered in ecstasy, but a voice of fear was warning her that to let Rick love her would be suicidal madness. It would bind him to her for ever. She would never be satisfied with anyone else. 'Oh God,' she moaned, sensing terrible disaster and having no power to prevent it. His other hand was moving tenderly down her spine, then resting on the roundness of her buttocks, stroking and massaging with tender authority as though she had belonged to him since time began.

'You are my woman, my mate,' he said hoarsely, emphasising the primitive message in the words with the soft animal growl of his tones.

She pushed her hands inside his T-shirt and stroked the warm toughness of his chest, toying delightedly with the sensitive male nipples, then her arms slipped around his back, holding him close against her with a sudden fierce protectiveness. 'Rick, darling,' she murmured, 'I feel so right with you: so safe.'

‘Safe! I’m not sure how happy I am about that!’ he said in a low voice, pushing his hands around her thighs and squeezing with more violence than tenderness so that she emitted a sharp, singing sigh.

‘Are you still feeling safe?’ he asked huskily.

Her heart was beating against her ribs like some frantic caged animal. She turned watery dark eyes up to his and parted her lips slightly, inviting him to cover them with his and cxplore her mouth with his tongue. Once again she felt that fierce connection between them. Just kissing him brought her to the point of ecstasy. ‘Yes, yes,’ she murmured. Her desire for him, her trust in him were so great that she felt free to surrender herself completely.

As their lips moved together so her body set out on a path of internal response. She felt herself awakening, unfolding delicately inside like a multitude of velvety fragile petals opening up to receive a priceless gift. He sat on the bed and pulled her to him inside his thighs, his hand reaching up and gently unfastening the buttons of the filmy blouse. It slithered softly to the floor to land in a small butter-coloured puddle around her feet. His hands moved gently, tracing the curve of her breast under the filmy peach satin.

Alexa felt her breath coming in great sobbing gasps. She wrenched down the thin satin strap and took his hand to place it on the naked skin. He pressed the rosy nipple, rolling it in his fingers — awakening a shower of internal electric sparks. Then his lips were stroking her throat, moving down to take the nipple into their tender protection. Her hands were in the tough thickness of his hair, rejoicing in its tensile strength, longingly tracing the outline of his skull.

Moments of languorous tenderness went by. Alexa felt a great pool of love and desire open up inside her; a pool whose existence she had only been dimly aware of until now. She grasped at his hair and pulled his face up to hers. She wanted his mouth again — to feel it joined to hers. She kissed him with dark ferocity as though she would swallow him up.

His response was to push her roughly down on the bed. 'OK. OK, baby. Time for me to take over. I'm a gentle man, but in bed I'll treat you like a woman — not a lady!'

Alexa gasped with astonishment as he began to pull the rest of her clothes off with little regard for their delicacy. It was as though he had shifted into a different emotional gear. The gentle light-hearted Rick she knew became almost savage in the intensity of his desire. And she could match him! In the dim base of her consciousness Alexa was amazed to learn that she too was a creature of deep animal passion. She could hear low purring growls in the air around — her own voice singing out for him to finish what he had started. The fusion of sensations was so strong that she began to weep with pleasure.

'Rick, darling — I love you, I love you!'

'Baby, baby — don't cry,' he soothed, stroking her sweat-soaked hair from her cheeks.

'So precious,' she murmured, 'such a wonderful precious memory to keep.' Her thoughts had spilled out loud into words she had never meant him to hear.

He froze. All movement ceased between them. She felt his body subside into terrible stillnes. 'My God,' he breathed, 'what did you say; a memory — is that what you said?'

'Yes,' she moaned, 'a memory, what else can it be?'

'You don't mean that!' he said roughly.

'Oh darling,' she wept, 'I do.'

He grasped her shoulders and shook her fiercely like a terrier shakes a rat. 'So this is just a 'one off' and then it's good-bye Rick — on your bike. Is that it?' His voice trembled with rage. 'Do you think I'm a machine Alexa, something you can switch on to gratify your undoubtedly hungry body — and then discard? Do you think I have no feelings?'

'No. Rick, please listen!'

He was pulling away from her, searching for his T-shirt, wrenching it back on in a crumple of inside out hem and neck and sleeves. 'Hell!' he cursed.

'Rick, let me explain.'

'Shut up,' he snapped. 'Don't make things any worse. If you give me that line about being a promised woman, God help me I don't know what I'll do to you.'

'But I am,' she said in despair. A stab of remorse shot through her. It was as though Royston's face was looking down at her, desperately wounded and disapproving to see the woman he trusted lying there naked with her limbs spread out and another man on the bed beside her.

'When are you ever going to see,' he said, 'that to marry that cold-eyed snake is sheer, maniacal disaster?'

She sprang up at him, digging her

nails into his neck.

'Don't be stupid,' he snarled, 'however evenly matched we are mentally, you won't win a stand up fight with me.'

'I don't care. I just want to hurt you,' she spat at him.

'You want to hurt me because I've upset your nice, cool emotional existence. That's it, isn't it?'

'Yes, as a matter of fact it is. I was fine before you came along and now I'm going to be miserable for ever,' she wailed.

'Well that's your funeral,' he said. 'There's absolutely no reason for you to be miserable. Just accept that you belong with me. That's all you have to do. It's simple.'

'Oh God, what a mess!' she whispered. 'Are you leaving now, Rick?' she asked stupidly as he rooted in his pocket for the keys to the bike.

'I can hardly stay when there's another man on guard inside that beautiful head of yours can I? Why don't you phone him Alexa? He'll be back from his dinner now, a fat contract in his pocket. No doubt he'd love to come and make a little up-tight love to his future wife. Finish what we started?'

Alexa stared at him.

'Or perhaps he's never made love to you,' he ground out. 'That wouldn't surprise me either. But I wouldn't have thought it made much difference one way or the other.'

'My God' she cried, 'your sexual ego must be colossal.'

'No — just realistic,' he told her coolly. 'And don't kid yourself Alexa, you're a very basic, sensual woman under those smart little suits of yours. Royston won't keep you happy for more than a couple of years. You'll be searching desperately for a lover to keep you satisfied. You're a 'natural' in bed — up to all sorts of little tricks that would make the right sort of man very happy indeed. I bet you never use them on him, do you?

Probably never knew you had them?'

Alexa had a flashing recall of that first day they met. Rick had been right to ask if she was afraid. It was not him she had need to be afraid of — but herself — the dark, passionate side of her nature which she had always kept locked away. 'Get out, get out!' she screamed in fury. With a dark throb of pity she pictured Royston; so considerate and hesitant in his love-making that she was sometimes prompted to wonder if he would ever get round to the point at all.

Rick was at the door now. He turned and looked at her. She shivered in her nakedness. He walked back into the room, picked up the soft white towelling wrap on the chair by the bed and slipped it around her shoulders. He bent down and laid his lips on hers, gently — very gently. 'You are my mate,' he said in low, tender tones. 'You belong with me, always — whoever else you may or may not sleep with or marry. Just remember that Alexa.'

She lay in trembling silence, hearing the outer door thud, listening to the waning note of the bike in the still night air.

5

The birds were singing with their morning-clear chiselled phrases as Alexa swam up into consciousness to find that the picture of Rick immediated slotted itself into the forefront of her brain. Her sleep had had a drugged quality about it and now she sought frantically to shake it off. She felt as though she were in ruins. Looking in the mirror she was alarmed to notice the dark blue crescents under her eyes. There were the beginnings of bruise marks on her shoulders and thighs. Thank God they, at least, could be covered up with clothes. She dabbed on some make-up and sprayed on Diorella — a daily ritual that she hoped might bring the return of a grain of sanity.

She made coffee and stood sipping the soothing warmth as she stared out into the velvet spring greenness of the garden. Birds cruised in the sky, the trees shook with wind, their new leaves swinging like lacy drapery. The world seemed to be going on in a surprisingly normal fashion. Yet Rick's face still floated in her mind's eye. His touch lingered all over her body. She admitted to herself that she wanted him more than anything, that she would never be able to have enough of him. She hated her own weakness.

Looking at it dispassionately she saw herself as a rather silly woman hovering on the brink of a crazy affair with a handsome young man in her employ. How she had always despised the men she knew who lusted after their secretaries and the pretty girls in the typing pool. She was no better than them, just as weak — blown about like a sapling in the rushing torrent of physical desire. Rick was very beautiful, there was no doubt about that, and full of sexual energy, skill and bravado — all of which was intensely exciting. But he had sprung from nowhere. She knew nothing about him. He was like a fairy prince who might suddenly turn into a frog. He was a lovable, darling rascal, a rake, a vagabond. She had no wish to be locked into vagabondage.

The phone rang.

'Alexa,' Hope's voice enquired solicitously, 'are you O.K.?'

'Yes — yes, of course.'

'It's nearly ten o'clock. I was worried about you.'

'What? Oh hell, I'll be there right away!'

Alexa moistened her lips. She suddenly remembered that the keys to Mr Armitage's precious purchase were still in her bag. She and Rick had completely forgotten about them in last night's wild excapades. 'Hope,' she said cautiously, horrified to think of her business and its tangible assets mirroring the chaos of her own inner turbulence, 'is everything . . . all right?'

'What?'

'That sage-green Jaguar, is it

. . . safe?' The car was a Pandora's box of tricks, every conceivable extra, trip computer, cruise control, electronic stereo cassette, air conditioning. She could imagine all this delicate equipment wickedly stripped from the vehicle, vandals disembowelling it in the night and leaving the entrails scattered over the road.

'Of course it's safe. Rick's just polishing it now.'

'Fine.' Alexa drew a deep breath and spoke briskly. 'I'll see you in a few minutes.

The important thing, the *only* thing that mattered, she mused as she sat behind the wheel and allowed the car to show what it could do regardless of speed limits, was to regain control — control of her work, control of her emotions, control of her life. She was not going to be blown off course by some dizzy infatuation with a rootless, virile, sexy young man. Having thus reduced Rick to no more than an assembly of throbbing muscles and a pair of dancing blue eyes she drew up outside her premises like Cleopatra entering Rome and stepped from the car with impressive dignity.

Rick was in the road, heavily engaged with the sage-green Jaguar. The dancing eyes were already on her, watching her with rapier sharp interest so that the back of her calves felt soft and liquidy. It did not surprise her to discover that Rick was not a man to brood and sulk. In fact his open cheery greeting was almost a disappointment, suggesting that his view of the evening was sanguine to the point of light-heartedness, whereas she felt that she had been broken into little pieces.

He straightened up from his attentions to the rear wing of the car and smiled at her — straight into her eyes. She felt the force of his greeting as strongly as though he had hit her with the flat of his hand.

'Good morning Rick,' she said determinedly, keeping her eyes fixed on the gleam of the car's green metal cladding and avoiding further confrontation with the disconcerting glint of his appraisal. 'You seem to have your work all organised as usual,' she muttered, her face flaming with the recollection of her naked body under his just a few hours previously.

'Yeah — plenty to keep me out of mischief,' he grinned, 'but I think we should talk later,' he said evenly.

'Well — I don't know. It's going to be very rushed today.'

'There'll be time,' he told her calmly, letting her know that he was calling the tune and there was to be no escape.

She started to hurry away.

'Alexa,' he called, 'can I have the keys — the ones I came to get last night?'

She reached into her bag, reflecting on the way in which this innocent little bunch of keys had wreaked havoc in her life.

'Thanks,' he smiled, 'we forgot all about them didn't we. Got side-tracked?' His eyes mocked her.

'Yes,' she said in chilly tones.

'Everyone is permitted their share of mistakes in life Rick, even the most level-headed of us.' Hoping that would put him firmly in his place she made for the shelter of her desk before he could unnerve her further.

'Royston's rung three times,' Hope said, looking at her sternly over big round tortoise-shell glasses. 'I think you'd better call back before serious hostilities commence!'

'Oh heavens!'

'Do you need coffee,' Hope asked, 'aspirin — brandy? You look decidedly rough Alexa. It's nice to know you're not perfect after all. Quite cheers me up!'

'Oh, don't you start. I couldn't stand it — and I'll have an aspirin please.' She dialled Royston's number with quivering hands.

'I called you late last night, three times,' he reproached her, 'there was no reply.'

Fury chased through Alexa's brain. Men! They thought they had a God-given right to sit like judging angels on what you did with your life. She could have expected that he would be conciliatory, full of apologies for his neglect. Instead he sounded faintly accusing, as though explanations were required of her.

'I was out,' she said softly.

He was already continuing with his theme. 'I can see that you would be upset but there was no need not to answer . . . ' Suddenly the words bit into his understanding. 'You were out?' he said incredulously.

'Yes. It was my birthday. I was all ready to go out — and so I went!' she told him with bright challenge.

'By yourself?' he asked sharply.

'No, with a friend. Did you get the contract?' She asked quickly before he could follow up her suprising revelations.

'No.'

'Oh darling, I *am* sorry.' That at least she could say genuinely.

'Yes, so were we. All that aggro for nothing.'

She grimaced in silent agreement.

'Look, I'll have to fly,' he told her, 'I'll pick you up this evening at seven.'

At the end of a hectic morning Alexa reflected that having an absorbing occupation went some way towards repairing shattered spirits. Being heavily in demand from the telephone and a steady stream of week-end customers also kept her firmly out of Rick's way. She was beginning to realise that she would very soon have to make important decisions about expanding the business, taking on new staff, ploughing in some hefty capital.

She telephoned Morris. 'I think I'm ready to talk some more,' she informed him, remembering their last meeting on that fateful day when Rick had erupted into her life.

'Good, I'll come round to your place next week. I'd like to look at the stock and I'm also due for changing my car. Kill two birds with one stone, eh?'

Alexa warmed to his blunt decisiveness. She was also touched and flattered that he wanted to buy a car from her. Royston steadfastly avoided putting the Wentworth fleet account in her hands, which was beginning to be wounding. She pulled herself up, sharply aware that her silent criticisms of her fiancé were becoming troublingly frequent.

Hope was persuaded to leave at four, protesting that there was still a lot of work to do. 'It's Saturday,' Alexa told her authoritatively. 'You've got a daughter to look after.'

'No, she's away this week-end with a friend. They'll be fully occupied with the Top Forty and a selection of adolescent boys with terminal acne. I'm free as a bird.' She grimaced seductively.

'Well, fly away then!' Alexa laughed.

Later on when the phone had subsided into silence she peered cautiously out of the window. Rick was nowhere to be seen, but his bike was propped up on the wall as usual. Could she manage to escape before he cornered her for his talk? She began to gather her things together stealthily like a teenager preparing to slip out of the house in full make-up without her parents seeing.

Rick appeared from the showroom door shrugging on his anorak. Even in early June the air was still sharp. There was a fresh breeze teasing the pinky-white tentacles of blossom on the late flowering cherry tree further down the road. Its branches swayed and bobbed cheerily.

A tall, slim blonde girl in a tight knee-length leather skirt and a bulky scrunchy-knit sweater was walking down the road, her arms laden with carrier bags. Alexa saw Rick look towards her — smile, wave and call out. Immediately her attention was riveted. With sickening fascination she watched as the girl moved close to Rick, stood laughing up at him and chatting animatedly whilst Rick in turn laughed back and swung the bags into the bike's carrier handing the girl the spare helmet Alexa herself had worn the previous evening. They both jumped on the bike, the girl enclosed Rick in her arms and then they were gone, only a thin blue tube of smoke remaining to mark their departure.

Alexa stared out of the window, her knuckles whitened with agitation as she clutched the frame. The events of the last few minutes appeared unreal. She willed them not to have happened but with sickening resignation she accepted that they had. She had a sharply venomous desire to pursue the couple in her Jaguar and fling the girl off Rick's bike, away from the crazy, she moaned to herself. Only an hour ago I was doing my best to keep out of Rick's way and now I'm longing and longing for him to come back and tell me all he's feeling and I'm insane with murderous jealousy because some girl has got a lift home on his bike. For surely there was no more to it than that. Please God there was no more to it than that.

With her emotions distressingly shredded and scrambled she returned home and attempted to compose herself with the performance of routine tasks, straightening cushions, rinsing out cups and glasses, taking a shower in preparation for dining out with Royston that evening. The bruises on her skin were deepening into dark grapey-black splodges. She touched them with fascinated tenderness, these marks of Rick's violent, abandoned loving. She wanted to preserve them for ever.

Royston arrived with an orchid in a plastic box — and a dark frown of sternness in his eyes. He kissed her perfunctorily, handed over the rigid, suffocating flower and came straight to the point. 'Alexa, someone saw you last night!'

Her heart leapt like a somersaulting tropical fish. 'Oh yes,' she said, trying to sound unruffled.

'At a wine bar,' Royston continued with heavy disapproval reminding Alexa of a disillusioned, world-weary headmaster.

'Yes?'

'With that scruffy-looking fellow who washes your cars!'

White hot anger exploded in a million fragments through Alexa's head. 'It's very difficult to be smart when you do the sort of work Rick does,' she said, pointedly observing the peach-like softness of Royston's hands with their white-rimmed finger nails.

'I shan't bother to argue about that,' Royston informed her coldly. 'The important issue is the fact that you were seen out with him — apparently having a very nice time.'

'Am I supposed to feel guilty?' Alexa asked through the tremble of rage which numbed her to all other emotion.

'Need you ask,' Royston said in glacial tones. 'Barry Cryer saw you,' he went on with heavy reproach. 'Our golf captain!'

Alexa remembered the polished, silver-haired man who had observed her with such interest in the wine bar. The mean, sneaky, traitorous tell-tale, she thought contemptuously. 'Oh dear,' she said sarcastically, 'that would be truly embarrassing for you, Royston. No doubt the story will have been disseminated down from the captain to all the little golf club ratings, eager for a nice bit of gossip.'

'Exactly,' Royston agreed with a raised voice, 'that's exactly what will happen. People will laugh behind my back.'

'Well — let them. Does it matter?' Already a cold trickle of doubt was cooling Alexa's rage. Perhaps it really was a terrible thing she had done, to be seen out in public with Rick. Perhaps that was even worse than taking her clothes off in the desperate need to feel Rick's wonderful, gentle hands on her naked body. A fresh wave of longing heat spread through her in harmony with the evening sunlight which she could see sweeping over the lawn outside. Her anger dissolved and she felt sick with guilt. 'I'm sorry,' she said in a low voice of misery, 'it was a stupid thing to do and I can say, from the bottom of my heart, that I never wished to humiliate or hurt you in any way. Will you please just accept that and not say anything else about it?' She looked pleadingly at him, twirling the little pearl earrings in anxiety and plucking at the neckline of her neat black dress.

'I really don't think I can let the matter rest there,' he said heavily. 'I'm very concerned about the way you're behaving at the moment.'

She turned swiftly away, not wanting to meet his eyes. Her glance fell on the flowers Rick had given her at the beginning of the week, still full of life and colour although past their first dewy freshness. Thinking of the warm, exuberant generosity that had prompted his giving them to her made her want to break down and weep. She had felt so good that day, truly light-hearted and joyful — and now everything was grey and desolate and dreadful.

'Ever since that Markland fellow

came on the scene. That's it isn't it?' His voice echoed with disdain.

'No! No!' She would never admit to Royston that Rick meant anything serious, that he had the power to destroy her equilibrium. She had not admitted it in full honesty to herself. 'It's work,' she protested frantically, 'I'm so busy!'

'You can't go on like this, Alexa. I keep telling you. Being in business is a hard life. You've got to be tough.'

'I *am* tough!'

'Yes, but how long can you take it? It's O.K. for a few years. You've been very successful, but do you have the long-term stamina?'

'Yes,' she cried, 'yes, yes, yes!'

'You are getting hysterical,' he said coolly.

'So would you be,' she screamed at him, 'if you were constantly having to prove yourself and justify your actions.'

He stared at her grimly. 'You need a real break. A holiday. Time to sort yourself out.'

'Oh, for heaven's sake, Royston, stop talking to me as though I were a precious, wilting little woman.'

'But you *are* only a woman!'

'Only!'

He faltered, tried to make amends. 'Well — you are a woman. It's hard for women in business. I make no apology for saying that. I'm simply concerned for your well-being. I really do think you should take things easy. Try to slow the sales turnover down a bit. After all, you've got the wedding to plan. Women love that sort of thing, don't they? You need time to enjoy all that.'

Alexa was beginning to wonder if he was right after all. Perhaps she *was* overstressed, becoming temperamental and giving everyone a hard time. She felt so weary that all she wanted to do was lay her head on the sofa cushions and go to sleep. 'Royston,' she asked, her voice low with feeling, 'if you think you've made a mistake — say so now. I won't make things difficult — and I'm sure you'll find someone else much nicer than me to marry!' She thought how strange it was that one said the most ludicrously crass things in moments of deep stress and also noted how amazing it was that she could be suggesting parting from Royston with so little real feeling.

To her astonishment his face crumpled up as though he were going to howl like a whipped dog. 'Oh God, I couldn't bear it, Alexa. I couldn't bear it if we broke up. Please, please don't say things like that. We'll make a go of it: I know we will. I need you.'

Thunderstruck pity flooded through her. How could she even think of breaking with him, of letting him down so dreadfully. She took his arm tenderly. 'Don't worry,' she soothed, 'don't worry any more. It will all be all right. We'll go out now to that beautiful Grensham Hall and have a lovely dinner and let the whole world know that everything is fine between us.'

* * *

Alexa stared moodily at the telephone and wondered if ten a.m. on a Sunday morning was too early to call Hope. A sleepy voice came on the line. 'Huh?'

'Hope, can I come round?'

'What?'

'I'm in a state!'

'Give me half an hour to put clothes and coffee on and I'll be waiting with bated breath!'

The June morning was filled with the sound of church bells as Alexa pulled her car up outside Hope's house.

'Drink that,' Hope instructed, handing her a cup of strong, freshly brewed coffee. She curled up on the sofa, tucking her short legs up and reminding Alexa of a plump cuddly kitten. 'What's the problem?' she wondered, smiling good-naturedly at her boss.

Alexa paused.

'I'll bet you don't feel like telling — now you've got here!'

Alexa laughed. 'You're right. I just needed some company — female company,' she added pointedly.

'Mmn, have you quarrelled with Royston?' Hope asked baldly.

'Yes.'

'Broken it off?'

'No.' Alexa tapped a fuchsia-coloured finger against her teeth. 'You don't like Royston do you, Hope?'

'I'm not convinced that he will make you happy,' Hope said worriedly.

Tears sprang into Alexa's eyes. 'I don't know what to think any more,' she said, putting her head in her hands. 'Everything's so confused.'

Hope waited patiently.

'What was your husband like?' Alexa asked softly.

'Nice, reliable, good-tempered. A cuddly, considerate lover as well.'

'What on earth went wrong?'

'He fell in love with someone else, a girl of twenty. She was carrying his child when he left me. He was an honourable sort of man, would never have let the girl down or kept her as his mistress.'

'Oh Hope! How sad for you. I never

knew it had happened like that.' Alexa was warm with sympathy.

Hope chuckled and shrugged. 'I never say, unless someone asks. Life went on. I had the house, my Open University course and my job with you.' She smiled wistfully then swerved her lips into a great wide grin of wickedness. 'And I gave myself permission to have lovers!'

Alexa's lips quivered with amusement. 'Will you marry again?'

'No.' Hope put her coffee down and considered. 'Well, I might,' she said slowly, 'but I would only go into it blindly and passionately because I just couldn't bear not to be with the guy forever. If I had to think rationally — then I'd stay single. A variety of lovers can be very pleasant. Are you shocked?'

'Yes, a little.'

'So, there we are. I'm just a creature of passion. Little, plump, middle-aged me. Who would believe it?'

'But — what about security?' Alexa wondered.

'What about it? Who's got it, total security? No-one.'

'I suppose not.' Alexa smoothed down her white linen jeans thoughtfully. She looked at Hope who looked back steadily. She knew that a portrait of Rick hung behind both their eyes. But she did not think she could bear to start on that dangerous topic, not even to Hope.

'More coffee?' Hope smiled.

The sound of a motor-cycle roaring up the road shattered the silence.

Alexa's heart pumped as though it would burst out of her chest.

Hope's face softened. 'That'll be Danny,' she said.

Alexa listened as she opened the door. 'Where have you been, you naughty boy?' she heard Hope murmur. 'It's been two weeks.' There was a long pause, soft little chuckles of pleasure.

'Who's is the classy car outside then?' A man's voice asked eventually. 'You got a rich visitor?'

'Yes, come and meet her!'

The man was young, very young, no more than early twenties. He wore old jeans, a distressed leather jacket and a day's growth of beard. His eyes followed Hope as she moved across the room; followed her as though she were the most desirable and adorable woman on earth. She pushed him down on the sofa and patted his cheek indulgently.

'I was just going,' Alexa said with tolerant amusement.

Hope winked as she let her out, then pressed her hand warmly. 'Any time — if you need an ear. Just call me!'

Alexa felt vaguely comforted as she drove away yet she was not quite sure what conclusions to draw from Hope's casually observed philosophical tit-bits. Taking one's emotional life by the throat might work for Hope — it would not necessarily work for Alexa who had always got her thrills from her business risks.

* * *

On Monday morning she checked out the account books, making sure they were up to date for Morris to inspect. She wandered around the showroom, stroking the shiny metal of the cars and mentally picking out one or two vehicles which she thought might suit Morris's purse and pocket. Rick had been working outside. She had observed him from her office. He came in now, his blond hair flying in all directions, his blue eyes sparkling, his big frame strong and reassuring. Alexa felt herself melt with warmth. Oh hell, she thought irritably, is this what one has to put up with when living through an infatuation, feeling as though paradise is imminently obtainable each time the damned guy walks in the room.

'Hi there!' His glance was warm and quizzical.

'Hi. Had a good week-end?' she asked mechanically, miserably picturing the blonde girl wriggling herself up against him and stroking his cheek at every available opportunity.

'Yes. And you?'

'Oh lovely,' she said in a high-pitched brittle voice. 'Look Rick, I've got my accountant coming in later on. He wants to look at a car; what do you think we should direct him towards?'

'That one,' he said without hesitation, pointing to a sober, claret-coloured Rover. 'Accountants like good value for money, something a bit special but nothing flamboyant.'

Goodness, he was always on the ball. 'Yes, you're right Rick,' she said reflectively.

'Aren't I usually?' he suggested meaningfully.

'Well, about cars anyway,' she said hastily.

'Really,' he drawled. 'I think you underestimate me. We haven't had our talk yet Alexa. I haven't forgotten. You're not getting off scot-free!' He turned swiftly and left her to digest this disturbing news. Foreboding and elation chased around her innards but as she sat later facing Morris he would never have guessed at her inner turbulence. She was the essence of cool, sophisticated professionalism.

'I don't know how you're managing to produce this turnover,' Morris stated bluntly, 'with such a small staff.'

'We can't do it for much longer,' Alexa agreed.

'So what *are* you going to do?'

'Two options,' Alexa said crisply, 'inject more capital of my own if the bank will give the go-ahead, or find a partner who will bring in assets, security and an extra pair of hands.'

Morris pressed the tips of his fingers together. 'Mmn — business partners are like marriage partners — hard to find and requiring a good deal of nurturing. Have you someone in mind?' he wondered with a sharp glance.

She shook her head, although Rick's image was, as usual, firmly trapped behind her eyes. But that was impossible to consider. Rick was penniless — and besides he was dangerous. Yet in so many other ways he would make an excellent partner. 'No,' she said firmly. 'Go ahead, Morris, and approach the bank for me. We'll get an agreement in principle and then we'll get down to figures later.'

'Right!' Morris's eyes gleamed with appreciation at her rapier-like decisiveness. 'Well then, let's go and look at all your four-wheeled goodies and see what you can tempt me with!'

She invited Rick into the showroom to help, noting with pleasure that the two men took an instant liking to each other so that when Hope called her to take a phone call she had no hesitation in leaving the two of them together.

The caller was a woman with a voice the texture of chocolate soufflé. 'You don't know me, Miss Lockton,' she said, 'but I've heard about you. I'm Pattie Maxwell, co-director of Front Line Fashions. I've just been given the go-ahead to buy in a fleet for our reps — and there's nothing I'd like better than to place the account with a woman who knows what she's doing. Can we talk serious business together some time?'

Excitement fizzed in Alexa's head. 'Of course,' she said coolly.

'I know you're only a small firm. You can handle it can't you?' The query was delivered with the sharp thrust of a lance.

'I can handle it!'

'O.K. Give me a few days to put some details together and I'll get back to you.'

Gleefully Alexa replaced the phone on the handset. The dizzy thrill of trading had raised her spirits at a stroke. Who needs love, who needs men she thought jubilantly. How much simpler it would be to dispense with all the emotional turbulence associated with the opposite sex.

She descended the steps with springy strides. Morris and Rick were sitting in the claret-coloured Rover examining its host of instruments and laughing and chatting like old friends. 'How do you like it Morris?' she asked, annoyed to find herself flushing slightly under the beam of Rick's eyes. She could see the tiger-yellow flecks, startlingly brilliant in the golden shaft of sunlight that fell over his broad frame.

'Beautiful!' Morris declared, eyeing both her and the vehicle with warm appreciation.

'Get it out, will you Rick. I'll take Morris for a drive.' Alexa spoke with authority, avoiding Rick's glance, daring her heart to start behaving like an eager steeple-chaser.

'Knows his stuff doesn't he, that young man of yours,' Morris commented as he slipped the car into first gear. 'In fact you could do worse than talk to *him* about the direction your business is going in. Wouldn't surprise me if he had a few bright ideas worth listening to!'

'No,' Alexa murmured. 'It wouldn't surprise me either.'

'Make the most of him,' Morris grinned, 'go-ahead fellow like that won't stay in one place too long. He's on the way up, aiming high I'll bet!'

Alexa thought over his words later, realising the truth of them. Of course Rick wouldn't stay long. He was probably just using her business to gain experience — and who could blame him. It would probably be very good for her peace of mind if he *did* leave, if he bounded out of her life as swiftly as he had skidded into it. Yet the thought of his absence from her life filled her with desolation.

She did nothing to avoid a private conversation with him that evening, in fact she became actively hungry for his company. If the blonde girl came along to claim him she was not sure that she might not run out into the road and claw her eyes out. She could hear Hope gathering her things together. 'Did you have a good day yesterday?' she asked, remembering young Danny and his adoring eyes.

'We certainly did,' Hope said, lips pursed, eyes twinkling. 'I can't say I share his tastes in music but we get on rather well in other more vital respects!'

'You're shameless!'

Hope shook her head. 'Not shameless. Simply having the courage to take what life offers. There is a difference, Alexa.'

Later Alexa stood in reflection at the window observing the long evening shadows stretching beyond the trees and laying themselves in the road like silent black tentacles. Hope was nearly forty and she was having an affair with a man young enough to be her son — and obviously having a ball. That really was rather reckless Alexa judged. She could imagine that many people would feel shock and revulsion at the thought of such a relationship. Taking what life had to offer she mused. Taking a lover like Danny half your age, taking a lover like Rick with no roots, no stability, no permanence. It might work for Hope but she did not really think it could work for her — even laying aside the fact that she had a reliable, deeply serious fiancé to consider.

She went into the little washroom at the end of the corridor, combed her hair, applied fresh lipstick and straightened the collar of her blue and white candy-striped blouse. She felt in command of herself for the first time in quite a few days — able to steer her life back onto a normal course. 'Rick,' she called from the top of the stairs, 'would you come and see me for a moment?'

Almost instantly he appeared in the doorway, his face cheery and smiling as usual. He was a quite remarkably sunny-tempered man; she was unable to deny the affection she felt for him. 'Do sit down,' she said formally. 'Shall we have a glass of sherry, it's almost seven o'clock?' She kept a small stock of drinks in the cupboard behind her desk.

He gave her a long look. 'O.K. if you want to be nice and civilised, we'll sip sherry together. Better than nothing. I'll take what crumbs you throw in my direction.'

Alexa's hands began to tremble as

she poured the sherry into the sensible plump glasses she kept for office use.

Rick had a knack of creating an atmosphere of intimacy between them whenever they were alone no matter how hard she tried to engineer a psychological distance. He treated her with friendly courtesy when the customers were about — but the minute they had gone . . .

'Rick, that night we went out together,' she began decisively.

'Yeah . . . ?'

'I'd really like us to forget all about it please.' Her lips felt pinched and tight as she spoke.

He laughed openly in her face. 'Liking is one thing, being able to is quite another. Can you really forget all that happened, Alexa? Was it so very trivial and unimportant?'

She was silent, running her finger round and round the rim of the glass so it squealed. All her noble resolve dribbled away. She wanted to take Rick in her arms, drive him home in her car and lie warmly entwined with him in her bed. She wanted to take all his clothes off and lick every inch of his salty male skin. She sighed out loud. 'We shouldn't have mixed business with pleasure,' she mourned.

'I rather thought we were mixing pleasure with pleasure,' he observed drily. He stood up and came to stand close to her. She stepped back involuntarily and stumbled against the desk. His arm flew out to steady her. She found her eyes staring at his broad chest, her heart thundering out a message of desire.

The interview was not going at all as she had planned.

'Alexa,' he commanded huskily, 'look at me!' He hooked a finger under her chin and tipped her face up to his. 'Darling,' he said, 'it's no good pretending that we don't want each other. I can feel you wanting to make love with me, now this minute, without your saying a word. Why deny it? Loving is beautiful — isn't it?' To emphasise his point he bent and kissed her.

She started to form the word 'no' in her throat and on her tongue but his lips were already joined to hers, their tongues were winding sensuously together, the warm juices of their mouths mingling with exquisite sweetness.

His arms moved possessively around her. 'Alexa,' he murmured, 'Alexa.' The smell of his skin was in her nostrils making her warm and dizzy. Rick's fingers pressed into her back, rubbing their way with insistent authority down the firm straight line of vertebrae. Alexa thrust her hands with hungry urgency into his thick hair. She pushed her hips against him and they moved in sensual, rapturous rhythm. Her hands moved from the heavy warmth of his hair down over his neck and shoulders and onto the hard muscular back. She began to experience a sensation of melting as though she would merge and flow into him and they would become one being.

'My love,' she whispered, 'Rick, my only love.'

Rick pulled gently away and looked at her with deep tenderness. 'You say very beautiful things, Alexa — when you're in my arms,' he added chidingly.

'Yes,' she murmured, 'yes, but it's madness.' Her voice was heavy with despair. 'Beautiful madness!'

He bent his head down again but she turned sharply away. 'We mustn't let this happen Rick. This being together and . . . '

'Making love?' he suggested.

'Yes.'

'We fit,' he said flatly. 'We belong together.'

'No!'

'Give him up Alexa. Give Royston up.'

She stared at him in disbelief. 'Do you know what you're saying?'

'Yes.'

'Rick, do you think you can simply walk into my life, walk into my feelings, walk into my bed — just like that?'

'I'd rather walk into your heart,' he said softly. 'I want to fill your heart. Did Royston ever express such a desire?' he enquired with faint derision.

Alexa's silence was answer enough.

'No, of course he didn't. He's no good for you Alexa. And what's more, you'll be bad news for him.'

'What the hell do you mean?' she snapped.

Rick imprisoned her arm in a grip of steel. 'You'll have to be very gentle with him,' he told her mockingly, 'a passionate woman like you could have a guy like him clapped out in months!'

Alexa was tempted to strike him. 'I don't find that at all amusing,' she said in a voice of ice.

'No, neither do I. I find the prospect of you and him together very unfunny. He'll act like the perfect gentleman in bed; nice, regular, restrained love-making under the sheets in the dark. And you'll be the perfect lady. What alternative will you have? What a cosy, dreary life you'll have together!'

'Marriage is a very serious and important undertaking,' she said with dignity.

'Yes, far too important and serious to undertake when there is no passion to keep it glued together.'

'Sex is not the only consideration in life!'

'It's a pretty crucial one!'

It struck Alexa that Rick was the only man she had ever talked to about sex without acute unease. But then he was the only man she had ever felt free to really let herself go with. What the hell was she going to do to get out of this emotional mess?

'Alexa,' he murmured thickly, 'you've got to set yourself free, fly a little — not just in business affairs, but in those of the heart as well. You *can* do it!'

'No, I can't do it,' she whispered, 'I can't do it to Royston, can't hurt him like that.'

'You're a woman of your word,' he said caustically.

'Yes.'

'Alexa — darling, I understand that. I admire you for it. But you'll hurt him more to marry him. It won't last. It's doomed before you've even started.'

'I can't do it. I can't. I *can't*!'

Rick's fingers tightened on her arm, crushing the fresh bruises so that she winced in pain.

'You must,' he growled at her, 'you can't go through with this marriage, we both know that. Admit it to yourself, you've had real doubts for weeks haven't you? Haven't you?' he repeated, shaking her forcefully.

'Yes! No! Oh God — I don't know. Just go away Rick — please. Leave me in peace.'

'No, not until we get this sorted out.'

Her distress turned to anger at his presumption. 'Sort things out! What are you suggesting? What am I supposed to do? Ditch Royston so I'm free to have a wild affair with you?'

He stared at her. He seemed to be struggling to find words to convey his feelings.

An intense silence invaded the room and both their bodies jerked with alarm as the phone peeled out unexpectedly. Alexa picked it up and spoke automatically, 'Good evening, Lockton's of Arkenfield.'

The voice at the other end was faint. Alexa could only catch the odd word. 'I think it's for you Rick,' she concluded, handing him the phone.

'Hullo?' Rick's face crinkled into a questioning frown, then as he listened became decisive and full of purpose. 'I'll be right there,' he said, 'I'm on my way. Don't worry about a thing!'

Instinctively Alexa's arm had crept protectively around him as he listened, sensing that the call carried bad news. 'What is it darling?' she asked gently, the endearment proceeding quite spontaneously from her lips.

'I've got to go,' he said ruefully.

A flood of disappointment washed over her.

'That was Penny. She's in a bit of a fix, needs my help,' he explained.

Alexa sprang away from him as though a slice of lightning had burst between them. 'Penny! Who's Penny?'

'The girl sharing my lodgings,' he told her calmly.

Alexa recalled the smiling blonde with the long legs. She felt suddenly exposed and fearful as though someone had whipped away the safety net whilst she danced on a high wire.

'What's the matter?' he asked softly. 'You're not jealous are you Alexa?' His tone was just a shade provocative.

Alexa straightened her shoulders. Suddenly sanity returned. Things regarding the sexy, flirtatious Rick fell into place. She patted the phone. 'Saved by the bell!' she said sweetly. 'What a fool I've been Rick. What a blind fool. I've had sleepless nights thinking that there was something of importance between us, something that might even have persuaded me to turn my back on a whole planned way of life.'

She paused to glance at him with deliberate, glacial calculation. With measured, composed dignity she began to collect up her things — keys, bag, jacket. 'I was even beginning to have glimpses of a future for both of us, a future beyond a brief, heady, passion-driven affair. And what was holding me back? I never really understood until now. It was my good old female intuition wasn't it, warning me to beware of a man who is so abundantly loaded up with charm and sexual bravado; a man who can twist women around his little finger? Because a man like that is never satisfied with one woman is he?'

Her eyes blazed with challenge.

'Oh my God, stop it Alexa,' he said in a tight voice of anguish. He moved towards her.

'Don't touch me!' she cried, shrinking away with such powerful revulsion that he froze in horror. 'I'm not the sort of woman who likes to be pawed around by a guy who's so bubbling over with sexy urges it would take a harem to keep him happy. Count me out Rick.

Cross me off the rota. I never liked team games at school, always preferred to do my own thing. On my own. And I don't intend to change now!' She glared with harsh resolution into his bewildered face. 'And what's more I don't want to go through life at full emotional throttle all the time. It's too wearing!'

He pushed a hand through his hair and there was pain in the line of his mouth. 'Alexa, listen. Penny's just a friend — nothing more than that. For God's sake!'

But Alexa was in no mood to listen. She was stripped raw and desperately hurt. She wanted to fight back, to wound and humiliate. 'I don't believe you for one moment, but it really doesn't matter,' she said with icy scorn, 'because our passionate little playtimes are over. Finished. I don't want you to touch me ever again. Is that clear? And now I'm going straight back to the man who's going to marry me, who's never cheated on me or played around, who's always reliable, controlled and faithful.

Poor Royston, I've got a lot to make up to him!'

Rick looked at her with mute appeal, his characteristic confidence suddenly dimmed. If Alexa had stayed to observe him she would have been shocked to see the depth of vulnerability and despair ravaging his strong features. But she was already at the bottom of the stairs before she called out to him, her voice hollow with derisive mockery. 'Save your masculine charm, your oceans of sex-appeal, Rick. It looks as though you might need them later on. They won't be required any more with me, however. From now on any co-operation between the two of us will be strictly business!'

6

Edith Wentworth bent down gracefully and plucked a recalcitrant sweet wrapper from the immaculately manicured lawns which spread themselves around the Wentworth's family home like a great velvet skirt. At sixty-five Mrs Wentworth was glowing with fitness in the way that women are when their lives have been free from the grind of hard work and there has never been any question of shortage of money.

'*So* lovely to have a garden to stroll in,' she said, pausing with satisfaction beside a rose bed where hundreds of trees were neatly strapped to their supporting stakes. 'But we'll take coffee inside Alexa dear; the insects are such a nuisance out here.'

In the hush of the sunny drawing-room, carpeted with a Wilton so thick that it retained their footprints, Mrs

Wentworth poured coffee from an engraved silver jug. 'Now then, how far on are you with the dress dear?' she enquired, 'so lovely to have a wedding to plan!' She looked bright and expectant.

Alexa brought out the beautiful sketches Sarah Nichols had produced for her. The gowns were extravagantly romantic; full-skirted, small-waisted, tucked and pleated, some embroidered with tiny pearls.

'Oh! The things today are so lovely,' Mrs Wentworth exclaimed. 'We were married in the war you know; no silks and satins available then. But I did have a lovely cherry red suit.' She pronounced it 'si-oote'. 'So useful afterwards.'

Alexa stared at the sketches and felt tears rise up into her throat. Each time she imagined the reality of one of these wonderful gowns she thought of herself standing beside Rick, felt his strong arm move possessively around her . . . But since that evening when he had dashed off in Lancelot fashion to rescue a maiden in distress, she had renounced him utterly. She had communicated her wish to dissociate herself from him so strongly that even the ebullient, zestful, ever laughing Rick had been subdued. He got on quietly and unquestioningly with his work — and she got on with hers. She permitted no light-hearted exchanges between them and she avoided any situation where she might be thrown together with him alone. Sometimes she wished that he would leave Lockton's, although how she would manage without him she still could not imagine. She toyed with the idea of trying to replace him. Replace Rick! She might as well cut off her right arm and attempt to find a substitute to graft on. Her business couldn't do without him.

Whilst Mrs Wentworth inspected the sketches, Alexa's eyes travelled around the walls from which stern Victorian landscapes stared down; paintings of bleak windswept moorlands peppered with a few lonely sheep — now curiously imprisoned in elaborately carved and gilded frames. Alexa sensed that in the Wentworth household everything was orderly and proper and secure. She had always, in the past, found a deeply satisfying predictability about it all, but today the atmosphere struck her as oppressive rather than reassuring, as though there were not sufficient air to breathe.

Mrs Wentworth laid the sketches down on the coffee table and reached for a folder of snapshots. 'James's family,' she said fondly, 'there's Antonia with the baby!' Grandmotherly pride oozed from every inch of her. Her younger son James and his new wife had delighted her with the production of a son and heir just a few weeks previously. Alexa looked at the baby's crumpled face and wondered whether she too would be presenting Mrs Wentworth with such a trophy before long. James and his family seemed to Alexa to represent the highest ideals on family life. Antonia looked so wholesome and pretty and . . . well *good*. She could not imagine her being swept away on a tide of dizzy sexual longing — except presumably for James of course!

Under the pure and blameless eye of her future mother-in-law Alexa was yet again convinced that her brief heady relationship with Rick Markland had been both ludicrous and shameful. She felt stained and tarnished, a creature of desires who could not resist a strongly muscled forearm and a twinkling blue eye. In the midst of these troubling reflections Mrs Wentworth's phone began to ring.

'Excuse me dear,' she murmured lifting the receiver. 'Miss Lockton? Yes . . . Is it really necessary? Oh well . . . whom shall I say?' There was faint accusation in her eyes as she said to Alexa, 'It's for you. A Mr Markland. I really do think he might have waited.'

The blood roared and thundered in Alexa's ears as Rick's voice sounded over the line. 'Alexa, I'm truly sorry to disturb you.'

'It's all right,' she said softly, knowing there would be a genuine reason. In business matters she could trust Rick completely.

'There's a customer here wanting to buy the silver Lancia.'

This car had been on Alexa's hands for months. Just occasionally one bought in a vehicle like that. It took up showroom space, meant that money was tied up and was generally a bit of a headache.

'Oh marvellous,' she laughed. She felt life and energy begin to flow again in her veins. The combination of the excitement of a prospective sale and the prospect of working co-operatively with Rick acted like a tonic on her sunken spirits.

'He's got cash,' Rick was saying, 'no car to trade in. He's asking for a ten per cent knock-down on the price. Can I go ahead; he wants a decision now?'

A straight cash deal! 'Don't let him

escape,' she instructed quickly. 'Yes, go ahead Rick — we'll argue about the commission when I get back.' It was the first time she had spoken in such a warm, easy manner to him since the onset of their cold war. She replaced the receiver and smiled at Mrs Wentworth feeling like a new woman.

There was a silence and Alexa knew in a rush of understanding that Mrs Wentworth had been informed of the birthday adventure with Rick, whether via Royston or the golf club gossip circuit she could not tell.

Mrs Wentworth, however, was too much of a lady to broach the matter openly. She said, 'Alexa dear, we are all very much looking forward to having you in the family. It has been so hard for Royston to find a really suitable, worthy kind of girl — and I make no bones about saying that. We regard you as a quite exceptional young woman — and Royston has always had the highest of standards.'

Alexa swallowed painfully. Standards

People like her and the Wentworths must preserve their standards. She understood that Mrs Wentworth would be entirely revolted to think of her even entertaining the idea of a sordid little affair with the rough and ready young man who washed her cars. She hated herself for thinking of Rick in that way. But perhaps that was the stark truth when one really got down to it. Cutting across the boundaries of money and social status was usually a complete disaster where long-term relationships were involved.

Before she left Mrs Wentworth slipped an engraved gilded invitation card into Alexa's hand. 'You haven't forgotten dear have you, Ronald and I celebrate our Ruby Wedding next month?'

'No, no — of course I haven't forgotten,' Alexa reassured her, with a sense of being irretrievably sucked into the Wentworth family as a mote of dust is drawn up into a vacuum cleaner.

* * *

In the offices above Lockton's showroom festivities were proceeding. Alexa found Hope and Rick clutched gleefully in each other's arms capering around like kids let out of school unexpectedly.

'Sorry,' said Rick, disentangling himself swiftly, 'just celebrating my sale.'

'Yes,' Alexa said drily, examining the brown envelope on her desk which bulged with fifty-pound notes. It was hard to be cross. She had done a little dancing herself in the past when a difficult sale had been pulled off.

Later on when Hope had left and the telephone had fallen silent, Rick came in quietly as she sat behind her desk methodically going through the inevitable, relentless paperwork. 'Alexa,' he said gently, 'would you be happier if I handed in my notice?'

The room seemed to shimmer and dance in front of her eyes. She felt weak and dizzy.

'Sometimes I think you really hate me,' he said.

She shook her head slowly. 'No — I need you, Rick.'

There was a long moment of silence. They both knew that the comment had a meaning that extended beyond business matters.

'Yes,' he remarked sadly, 'I think I can dare to believe that — even after these last few days.'

She hesitated. 'It hasn't been easy for either of us.' She fingered the gold choker at her throat, anxious and uncertain as to what to say next.

He smiled, but his blue eyes were full of hurt. 'I never realised what it was like to want something very much and see it just slipping uselessly away,' he told her with dull resignation.

She closed her eyes in grief. She wanted to take him in her arms and comfort him — give him all that he wanted. Instead she said briskly, 'We'll get over it Rick. We'll be fine. I've got Royston and a good marriage in front of me and I've got the business and security . . . ' She ran out of soothing platitudes.

'And what have *I* got?' he asked in a low voice.

'Everything! Youth, energy, charm, brains . . . and a wonderful way with women,' she added, trying to sound cheerful, 'what more do you want?'

'You!'

Panic clutched her heart. 'I'm trying to be sensible, Rick,' she protested faintly.

He was intent and watchful. 'Do you really want me to stay?'

'Yes, you're the best I've ever had. In fact . . . ' She paused, reluctant to continue the theme which had broken out on impulse. She twisted her pen thoughtfully in her fingers.

'What?'

'Well . . . if you had some money to put into the firm I'd be seriously interested in asking you to consider a partnership.'

A smile spread from his lips to

sparkle in his blue eyes. 'You really think I'm that good, you trust me that much?'

'Yes, yes I do.' She was puzzled at his reaction. He was obviously delighted, yet he seemed full of conflict — as though holding something back. 'Will you stay then?' she wondered.

'Strictly business?'

'Oh — *yes*!'

'I don't know,' he said slowly. 'I don't know if I can stand it.'

* * *

Royston was behaving very well indeed. Being a mature and experienced man he understood that a woman in expectant anticipation of her wedding — especially a wedding as grand and solemn as *this* one was going to be — was in need of careful handling. He took her to expensive dinners, to the theatre and to dinner parties at his friends' houses. He gave her long-stemmed roses wrapped in cellophane.

He never stayed too late at her flat or made undue physical demands. He chided her gently, as usual, for working too hard; but was prepared to accept that this was a delicate point with her and refused to enter into any serious discussions that might lead to arguments. He felt that there would be plenty of time for her to rest later on. He had noticed, among the wives of family and friends, a tendency to lose ambitiousness regarding a career when pregnancy and children came along.

* * *

Rick went up to the far north of the county to see Bess. She guessed everything. She said nothing. She knew that for the first time in his life there was something he wanted desperately but for some reason could not have. He must, at long last, be in love. What else in life would present him with such a baffling set of obstacles?

* * *

On the morning of the Wentworths' Ruby Wedding, Alexa had a long soak in a scented bath and then put on a dress of dark navy with a large white organza collar.

'You look absolutely stunning.' was Hope's comment as she laid the morning mail on Alexa's desk.

Alexa smiled faintly. She was not looking forward to the anniversary celebrations one little bit. She was anxious and resentful about taking time off work and she had just suffered the unnerving experience of observing Rick working outside, stripped to the waist and deeply tanned. Thick yellow bars of sunshine lay on his bare skin, the light curving gently around every line of the bone and muscle on his strong broad chest. There was a deep, boyish dent in the back of his neck, which gave him a curiously moving vulnerability despite his size and power.

How long could she bear this

wanting? How long could she hold him away from her?

At eleven-thirty she freshened up her lipstick and Diorella, checked that all was well with Hope, and walked out to the Jaguar. Rick looked up from his work on a white Mercedes Sport. She noted with sadness that his eyes were wary, that there were fine lines of weary resignation around his generous mouth. 'Have a good time,' he said politely.

'Yes — thank you,' she said stiffly.

'Just enjoy yourself,' he reassured her, 'we'll look after everything here.'

She smiled. 'Yes, you will — I'm sure.'

Rick gave her a long look. She could feel his spirit calling to hers across the gulf she had created. Turning swiftly she got into the Jaguar and accelerated down the road.

* * *

Edith and Ronald Wentworth's garden was already buzzing with people when she arrived. A marquee had been erected on the lawn and a splendid buffet was set out on long tables under the canvas. The guests strolled with drinks across the sun dappled brightness of the grass and under the distant trees Alexa could see the sunshine falling through the leafy branches to lie like a shower of freshly minted coins amongst the daisies.

Mrs Wentworth, magnificent in peony pink, advanced on Alexa. 'My dear,' she enthused, 'you look so elegant.'

'Here's my girl!' Ronald Wentworth boomed, bringing her a glass of champagne. 'How such a pretty head can carry business brains I'll never know. But you're a lady of leisure today,' he admonished. 'No bringing work to the party eh?'

'Royston will be here in a minute,' Mrs Wentworth whispered. 'He had a few important last-minute things to see to at work. You know how it is!'

Alexa felt a stab of annoyance. Mrs

Wentworth took her arm and introduced her to a number of guests. 'This is my daughter-in-law to be. She's such a busy person — so good of her to give up precious time to come to our little celebration.'

'Ah — a working woman,' one man said, eyeing her suspiciously.

'We women — our work is never done,' Mrs Wentworth rejoiced sweetly, by implication binding her own pampered existence and Alexa's struggles together at a brief verbal stroke.

Alexa circulated amongst the guests dutifully, soaking up the banalities and wishing the time would not crawl so slowly. She felt herself to be in a state of ripely wretched misery. She wished Royston would come, but when he finally appeared at the French window, scanning the crowd in search of her, she wanted to run away and hide.

'Sorry I'm late, darling. I'm so busy at present.' He passed a hand of exhaustion over his brow.

'So am I,' she reproached him. 'It was

really difficult getting away today.'

'Oh now don't let's quarrel,' he said softly, a watchful eye on the other guests. 'Have things been going badly for you? Are there problems?'

'Things have been going splendidly,' she told him firmly. 'Never better in fact.'

He took her hand. 'Could be time to capitalise on your success,' he ventured, 'sell out for a big profit. I know one or two firms who would be very interested in snapping Lockton's up.'

Alexa felt her mouth fall open in amazement. Royston's tone was unusually playful — but he could just be serious.

'Sell the business!' she exclaimed in distress. 'But it's only a baby; how could I think of selling?'

Royston ran a finger under her chin. 'You'll have other babies darling — you and me together.' He smiled. He was especially relaxed and happy today. Like his mother, he relished a grand occasion.

A blonde woman drifted across the lawn and came to stand beside him.

'Barbie!' He kissed her cheek. 'I haven't seen you for years.'

'Eight to be exact,' she said, glancing up at him from thick sable lashes. She appraised Alexa with interest. 'Aren't you going to introduce me?'

'Alexa, this is Barbie, an old family friend.' Royston was positively leering!

'Hey, not so much of the 'old'. I haven't hit thirty-five yet!' Barbie, slender to the point of emaciation, finished off her postage-stamp-sized prawn sandwich and said languidly, 'You're a lucky lady Alexa, I always hoped that Royston might look in *my* direction.'

Royston smiled with a mixture of embarrassment and gratification.

'You were snapped up too quickly,' he said gallantly, 'I never had a chance.'

'Oh dear,' Barbie drawled wearily, 'what splendid opportunities are lost along life's stony pathway.'

Alexa was painfully aware of the

nakedly seductive look Barbie was treating her future husband to, and registering his flattered smile she was tempted to scream.

Drawing in a deep breath, Royston said, 'I think I should circulate a little. I'll leave you two ladies together.'

Barbie regarded Alexa with a certain sceptical admiration. 'You've got your own business haven't you?'

'Yes.'

'Rather you than me. I tried being Superwoman for a while myself. Marriage, a career, a kid. It was horrific. Ended up in disaster and divorce.' She took the measure of Alexa's response. 'Am I being disgustingly tactless?'

'It's O.K.' Alexa said dully. At least Barbie's barbs represented an honest opinion. They were preferable to Mrs Wentworth's platitudes.

Barbie continued her theme. 'I've got friends still on the treadmill — rapidly progressing to a state of total collapse before they're thirty.' She shot Alexa a piercing glance. 'You ought to watch it.

You've got that care-worn look already.'

'I'll remember the advice,' Alexa said drily. 'And how do you spend your time, Barbie?'

'Searching for husband number two. Someone who likes being cosseted by a stay-at-home wife — and who pays all the bills!'

'I hope you find him,' Alexa murmured. She drained her glass of champagne, much as one would swallow aspirin to dull an insistent pain.

A white Mercedes rolled up the drive, awakening a sudden spark of interest in her weary head. She watched in surprised fascination as Rick eased himself from the driving seat and straightened his tall figure. He had pulled on a thin check shirt since she last saw him but even so in his jeans and trainers he stood out in sharp contrast to all the formally clad guests. He identified her instantly and came across the lawn with long loping strides.

'My, oh my — a latter-day Greek God alive and well in Arkenfield

Barbie commented in her lazy drawl.

Mingled pleasure and alarm jockeyed for position in Alexa's emotions. 'Hello Rick!' She looked up at him with anxious questioning.

Rick smiled in brief acknowledgement of Barbie, then said to Alexa, 'I'm really sorry to crash in on the party. I phoned but no-one's answering in the house. You've got to get back to Lockton's quickly!'

'Oh heavens.' She had visions of the place going up in smoke. 'Is something wrong?'

'No, but there could be an awful lot going right if you get back fast. Someone called Pattie Maxwell has just appeared. She's talking about a fleet order and wondering why the proprietress isn't around.'

'I'll leave you,' Barbie murmured tactfully. 'I can see that working has its compensations after all on occasions!'

Alexa barely noticed her departure. 'Pattie Maxwell! But she didn't have an appointment.'

'No, but she did make the effort to turn up.'

'Oh hell!' Alexa looked around at the elegant, faultless party knowing that her leaving would be a blight on the proceedings. Royston would be furious.

'Alexa,' Rick said urgently, shaking her arm, 'you've *got* to come!'

Royston had suddenly materialised by her side, his face dark with anger. 'What are you doing here?' he demanded, his eyes taking in Rick's work-stained clothes with disdain.

'Alexa is needed at Lockton's as soon as possible,' Rick said calmly.

'I think Alexa, not you, should be the judge of that,' Royston told him, 'you seem to be taking rather a lot on yourself for a chap who earns his living washing cars.'

Alexa winced. 'Rick is trying to be helpful,' she said quietly.

'Fair enough. But he doesn't come here and tell you what to do for goodness' sake,' Royston said irritably.

'He's come to give me advice,' Alexa

said firmly, aware of new reserves of strength with Rick by her side. She was able to deal with Royston with dignity and composure.

'There's a big order at stake,' Rick explained to Royston. 'If Alexa doesn't come now she might miss it.' His eyes sought Alexa's once more in urgent appeal.

'A serious, genuine customer will wait,' Royston announced coldly.

Memories of the customer who couldn't be made to wait on her birthday flashed through Alexa's mind.

Rick said, 'I think you should keep out of this Royston.' He spoke amiably but there was an undercurrent of challenge. 'I think this is a matter for Alexa to decide.'

Royston flushed. 'Who the hell do you think you're talking to? I ought to throw you out!' He observed Rick's broad frame, his powerful muscles and declined to pursue this particular tactic.

'Alexa, are you going to allow this fellow to walk in here and drag you off?

Where's your sense of what's right and proper, your sense of pride and respect?'

'With my business,' Alexa said, her voice deep with conviction. 'That's where all those admirable qualities belong — and that's where I'm going now. Please give my apologies to your parents. I'm sure they will understand.'

Royston stared uncomprehendingly at her. She suddenly saw him in sharp focus as though a skin had been peeled from her eyes. He presented himself, not as a reprehensible or bullying man, but a deeply conventional one, entirely bound by the rigid restrictions of his upbringing and life-style. He had, quite simply, never dared to break out, never been brave enough to take risks. Could she really go through with the marriage, she wondered, as she walked with Rick over the sun speckled grass? But on the other hand could she ever go through with telling him that they must call it off?

The Jaguar was trapped at the top o

the drive. She would have to leave it. She sat beside Rick in the Mercedes as he reversed out of the gateway and experienced a great rush of relief — as though she had been sprung from a trap. 'Oh God,' she smiled, 'I feel truly wicked!'

Rick grinned in approval. 'Who was the stringy exhausted blonde you were talking to? She seemed vaguely familiar.'

'An old family friend of the Wentworths apparently. She's searching for husband number two. He's got to be very rich with the ever open cheque book!'

'Ah, that explains the exhaustion. Guys like that are thin on the ground. What about good old Royston. Wouldn't he fit the bill — *pay* the bills, whichever way you prefer to look at it?'

Alexa could not stop herself laughing. 'That's a most improper suggestion, Rick.'

'I'm going to make another,' he said meaningfully, 'now that we're alone for the first time in weeks.'

'Stop it!' she said in agitation. She pulled down the sun visor and inspected her face in the mirror. 'Oh heavens, do I look drunk and dishevelled?'

'You look perfectly sober and impossibly desirable,' he said. A muscle flickered in his jaw under the golden tan.

'Don't start that again,' she whispered. She kept her gaze very firmly on the road ahead. Rick was driving very fast. But where were they going? Seemingly up on the moors. 'Rick, where are you taking me?' she asked in sudden panic.

'To a beautiful woodland glade,' he told her calmly, 'where I shall ravish you with exquisite protraction.'

'For God's sake, don't tease. It's not funny!'

'Oh, I'm not teasing.' He glanced towards her and she saw the purpose and determination in his eyes. A thrill of fascinated apprehension shot through her; to be pursued by a certain horrified suspicion. 'Was all that about Pattie Maxwell a complete fabrication?'

'Oh no, Pattie Maxwell's waiting for you all right.'

They were driving now along a narrow track running up into the dark forest that bordered the North Yorkshire National Park.

'Rick, you're mad. You've gone Crazy!'

'No, I've come to my senses at last,' he said coolly. 'I told Miss Maxwell that you were a very busy woman and that I wouldn't be able to have you back until two-thirty. I advised her on the most excellent restaurant in Arkenfield where she could have lunch. By my estimate, if I drive like a maniac, I'll get you back at two-fifteen. That leaves us with exactly fifteen minutes to spare doesn't it?'

He brought the car to a halt under the shadow of the lofty pines whose trunks were patched with silver-green moss.

The silence was complete.

He leaned slowly towards her. With

quiet purpose he ran his hand over the curve of her cheek.

She stared at him.

'You and I,' he said significantly, 'have a little unfinished business to attend to!'

7

Alexa stopped struggling and thinking about screaming as Rick's lips made contact with hers. Instead she put her arms around his neck and kissed him back with all her heart and mind and soul.

She began to feel reckless, a combination of the effects of the champagne and this totally unlooked-for opportunity to be alone with Rick.

She began to devour him like someone who has been on a starvation diet. She tore open his shirt and thrust her hands inside, pummelling the warm flesh with tender violence. Her fingers crawled into his armpits feeling the warm juice of his sweat and tingling with delight. Meanwhile her mouth attacked his as though life and death were at stake.

'Hey baby,' he murmured, 'leave just

a little of me for next time!'

She gave herself permission to act as the passionate woman she had always wanted to be. She forgot about time, forgot about Royston, about being a lady — even about the appointment with Pattie Maxwell. The whole of life was captured just here, here in this shining moment with Rick.

He gave a sudden velvety growl. 'I am going to be your man. The only man you will ever want. I'm going to wipe out every trace of Royston Wentworth, here and here and here,' he told her touching her breasts and hips and thighs, gently at first then without mercy.

'You are quite mad,' she sighed in ecstasy.

She was on fire. Her body screamed with longing for him.

She acquiesced to all the months of stored up wanting.

Then suddenly his hands were still, they no longer caressed her.

'Don't stop,' she pleaded in bewilderment. 'Please Rick, please!'

He shook his head. 'We need to talk. Now that you're desperate for me perhaps you'll listen to me for once.'

She sat up, flushed and trembling with shock. Her hand flew out and connected with his jaw. 'You rat, you bastard!' She was wild with wanting — and he was presuming to deny her.

'I'm tired of pussyfooting around, considering your delicate feelings.' Rick told her. 'Next thing I'll be a Royston look-alike — an overstuffed shirt covering an empty heart.'

'We've nothing in common,' she whispered in anguish, 'just bodies.'

'Is that what you really think?' he asked contemptuously. 'Any feeling you have for me is simply lust, sex, desire — something a bit dark and wicked? The cool business lady, she can distinguish between a little sexual thrill, but in no way is her heart ever to be involved? Her heart is driven by tax audits and annual turnover statistics. She permits herself a dull, sexless fiancé because he will never be any threat to that efficiently beating heart. He'll never be able to get into it — even if he wanted to!' Alexa tried to speak but he silenced her. 'You've got flair, drive and determination. That grey man with his grey, dead eyes will search them out and kill them. Because, you see, he doesn't want any competition. In no way will he permit his own staid, safe business style to be endangered.'

'Oh Rick, don't go on!' she cried in grief.

'You marry him and within a couple of years you'll be a spoiled suburban housewife patrolling an eight-bedroomed detached residence —having an elegant little dinner all ready for him when he comes home work-weary each night!'

'You're killing me. How can you be so brutal?'

'It's the truth isn't it. *Isn't it*?' He shook her hard.

'I don't know. Perhaps. Oh God!'

'Royston's no fool. I'll give him that. He's a high flier; he wants the very best — a woman who's beautiful, intelligent.

successful and rich. But not only that. His manly pride wants the satisfaction of seeing this superb woman give up everything she has achieved — just for him. Oh not straight away, but soon. I'll bet he's made a start already — 'rest a little darling, you're working too much, being in trade is hard for a woman . . . ''
He gripped her arm fiercely, daring her to deny it all.

She felt physically sick. No words came.

'Royston's still back in the dark ages when men thought that women were only playing at work until something else turned up — like a man!'

'Don't go on, Rick. I know all that.' Her eyes were big with hurt.

'Alexa, I know you think I'm a bit of a joker, but I take you very seriously. That's why I think you should be sitting behind your desk instead of drinking champagne with those fat cats!'

'And look what I'm doing now,' she remarked acidly, 'hardly very business-like.' She began to fasten up her dress.

'You haven't exactly put me in the mood for working, have you, Rick? Maybe you're just as bad as Royston — or worse. At least he wants my soul, *you* just want my body!'

With characteristic big-heartedness, Rick chose to ignore the taunt. 'You need your business.' he said in a low voice, 'you need it like you need air to breathe.'

Alexa swallowed. A great lump of feeling had risen in her throat.

High above, the trees waved their branches gently against the blueness of the sky and tiny jewelled birds darted through the air. She turned back to Rick. How well he understood her. How much she needed him.

'Darling,' he said tenderly, 'a guy who is jealous of your work and your achievements is about as much use to you as a legless jockey!'

She put out her hand and rested it, palm down, on his cheek. 'You see, I really did think he was a good man,' she said humbly, as though seeking Rick's forgiveness, 'a worthy man.'

She was surprised to see a sudden glitter in Rick's eyes.

'And I'm not a worthy man, is that it? I'm just a lousy, car-washing bum?'

Alexa stared at him, deeply hurt. 'How can you say that? I may have a lot of faults, I may have been blind and stupid, but I never thought any the less of you because of your job!' Tears sprang into her eyes. 'Never!'

'I'm sorry,' he murmured, 'truly sorry. I never believed that — it's just that I've been so desperate. The thought of your marrying Royston has nearly sent me off my head!'

Alexa realised how wrong and confused her thinking had been over these past months. Because Rick did not wear dark suits and say safe things, because he opened himself up to life and all its possibilities, because he dared to be fiercely honest, she had concluded that in some way he must be unstable and unpredictable. Whereas the truth was that she could trust him entirely; with her happiness, her self-esteem, her total being. Instinctively a feeling emanating from the very root of her told her that there was no need for rational consideration. Oh yes, Rick was attractive to women and responded to their admiration, but then she too responded to the admiration of other men. That was part of being a whole sexual person. There was nothing in all of that to work against the truth and depth of their feelings for each other.

The way forward seemed simple and clear.

She stretched out her right hand and pulled Rick's head towards her. She stuck her tongue playfully into his ear, then deliberately and slowly extended her left hand and removed the diamond cluster from her third finger. 'There,' she said, slipping it into her bag, 'will that do? Can I go back to work now please?'

Rick gave a great groan of delight. 'You miracle,' he said, 'I adore you, I adore you. I shall worship you for ever!'

'I should hope so. I should expect nothing less . . . from my man!'

They held each other for a while. She looked up into his face and saw that he was deep in thought. And he was troubled.

'Darling, what's the matter?' She stroked his arm. 'Is there something you want to tell me?'

A sigh shot through his chest. 'Yes.'

'Well?' she asked gently, thinking *oh God, not Penny-Long-Legs, has he something to tell me about her?*

He smiled, 'Give me time, just give me time.'

She gulped down her anxiety and they prepared to set off to Lockton's. Alexa tried to straighten her dress and hair. She had to search on the floor for her garnet and pearl pin.

Rick's hair looked as though it had got caught in a rotating fan and two of his shirt buttons were missing.

'Oh goodness,' she said, 'whatever will Pattie Maxwell think?'

'She'll think you've been exquisitely

bewitched and ravished in a dark woodland glade,' Rick replied, shooting the Mercedes out into the road and accelerating way beyond the speed limit.

* * *

'I think that's as far as we can go today.' Pattie Maxwell slid the papers on her knee into her ox-blood hide document case.

Alexa regarded her with interest, this woman with whom she had spent no more than one and a half hours, but who had probably set her business off on a wholly new and exciting road of expansion. If Alexa could come up with the goods that were needed and could raise the necessary capital for the venture, her whole pattern of trading could change. Pattie Maxwell had made it clear that a satisfactory performance by Lockton's on this deal would result in regular repeat business and the warm recommendation of the firm to a host of new customers.

Ms Maxwell, a tall dark lady in her sophisticated thirties, regretted that she could not stay on to take Alexa out to dinner. 'We must make sure to do that the next time,' she said with a warm smile from big brown eyes.

They met up with Rick as they walked through the showroom, making for Pattie Maxwell's company Porsche 924 which waited just outside the door. Her shrewd, liquidy eyes moved over Rick with undisguised admiration, lingering unashamedly over especial points of interest; his merry eyes, his sensual mouth, high tightly muscled haunches. 'Ah, I've already met Mr Markland.' she said to Alexa, 'you're lucky to have staff who can handle things so well in your absence!' She slid her sleek body into the car, tucking in the long legs with grace — and provocation.

'Hmn,' Alexa said, as the Porsche roared into life and vanished. 'Don't think I didn't notice that 'call me anytime' look she threw you. Did she leave you her number on an engraved card?'

Rick winked at her. 'Sorry to disappoint your romantic fantastising; she was fresh out of engraved cards — just wrote it down on the back of my hand in indelible ink!'

They stood together, laughing and teasing and totally at ease. Alexa felt no threat from Pattie Maxwell. No threat from any other woman now. She knew that she was right for Rick. She, Alexa Lockton, could make him happy like no-one else. And he, in turn, was her love, her friend, her equal, her true partner.

She had made up her mind to tell Royston tonight, although the thought of the interview filled her with dread.

Rick slid an arm around her.

'No darling,' she whispered. 'Don't touch me now — not until I've done this awful thing.'

'Hell. It's rotten for you. I wish I could help.'

'Well you can't. You're not the one he was going to marry!'

Rick drove her to the Wentworths' house and dropped her off tactfully outside the gates. 'I'll be waiting for you at my place,' he told her tenderly, 'come along as soon as you can. We'll have a special celebration.'

Alexa walked slowly up the drive, her Jaguar waited silently near the house. She wished that she could simply jump into it and drive away without having to go through the appalling task of jilting Royston — for she was sure that that would be how he would see her actions.

Mrs Wentworth opened the door, her demeanour uncompromisingly polite but noticeably distant. 'I'll show you into the study,' she said. 'Royston would like to talk to you on your own and we still have guests in the drawing-room.'

Alexa began to apologise for her sudden departure earlier on but Mrs Wentworth seemed not to hear and moved regally away. In the hushed, oak-panelled study, Alexa tried to stop herself pacing up and down like a caged tigress.

Royston did not come straight away. If he had wanted to make her sweat, he was certainly succeeding.

Suddenly he was in the room smiling down at her. In his eyes she saw a curious glittering triumph as though he had some little punishment up his sleeve, the administration of which he was going to savour. He did not speak, just watched her.

She moistened her lips. 'Royston, there's something I want to tell you.'

'Really. There's something I want to tell *you* first. It's rather important.'

Her heart thudded furiously. She stared at him, transfixed. 'What about?'

'About Richard Markland, that invaluable assistant of yours who seems to think he can work you from a little string as though you were a puppet to go where he pleases!'

'Oh don't let's go through all that again,' she sighed. 'I'm truly sorry about leaving early today but there was a very good reason.'

Royston continued to smile. He moved his face closer to hers. There was a look of greedy anticipation in his eyes. 'Let's forget about that regrettable little incident. My piece of news is far more significant.'

'Well for heaven's sake — tell me!'

He paused, like a torturer judging just where to place the hot needle for maximum effect. 'You've heard of Markland's Tools haven't you, Alexa?'

'Yes, of course.' Everyone in Yorkshire knew about Markland Tools. It was one of the biggest, oldest established businesses in the area. Still thriving, still expanding, still family-owned. Naturally she had heard of it.

'It never occurred to you to link up your precious car washer with the Markland concern?'

Astonishment drenched Alexa's thoughts. She began to see what he was getting at. 'You mean *my* Rick Markland is one of the family who own Markland Tools?'

'*Your* Rick Markland,' Royston said with sarcasm, 'is not only one of the family — he is Elizabeth Markland's only grandchild; heir to the entire company!'

Alexa struggled to comrehend and digest this news and all its implications. 'Are you sure? How do you know?'

'Barbie recognised him. She was at a reception last week at the Frenshams' estate. All the local big-wigs were there. Markland was escorting his grandmother. According to Barbie he looked rather different to the way we're used to seeing him; dark suit, tie, clean for once, hair combed — quite respectable in fact.'

Alexa felt a wound up through her body as though a knife had cleaved her. She stared at Royston, her face pale. 'You're revelling in this,' she said in a low voice, 'you're really enjoying it. Why? Why do you want to hurt me so badly?'

'I hate the guy,' Royston said with

venom, 'I hate his trendy laid-back approach to life, his scruffy good looks, his easy way with women.' He slid Alexa a glance of unmitigated triumph. 'Oh yes, I'd noticed that all right. Apparently he was quite wild when he was at Oxford, very popular with the ladies. No doubt he added you to his string of conquests for a while. But I think you'll find that he'll be off like lightning now the secret's out. You just wait and see.'

Alexa was stunned with hollow amazement. 'He worked so hard,' she said, trying desperately to absorb this new picture of Rick which Royston had been so delighted to spring on her.

'Work! He was just playing. He's an heir to a fortune. Markland's annual turnover makes Wentworth's look like pocket money,' Royston commented sourly. 'He must have had great fun amusing himself for a while in your little concern, probably had quite a few laughs up his sleeve.'

Alexa closed her eyes. Oh God that

hurt her. That really hurt her. Oh Rick!

'No, no — I don't believe that of him,' she said in anguish.

'Oh, come on — he's made a real fool of you. Of me, too, damn him.' Royston put out a conciliatory hand. 'Look, he'll clear off now to the green pastures where he belongs and you and I can settle down to a sane existence again. I'm not a vindictive man, I'm quite prepared to overlook your little errors of judgement — both in personal and business matters!'

Alexa straightened her spine and looked him directly in the eye. 'Like you, I too had something important to say this evening. It was going to be very difficult, but now that I see how little true warmth there is between us it seems much easier.' She took the ring from her bag and gave it back to him with careful solemnity.

'You're ditching me,' he said as awareness dawned.

She rose with calm dignity although her limbs quivered with agitation. 'No.

I'm just avoiding the two of us making a terrible mistake. I'm doing you a good turn. You'll see that once you get over the shock and stop worrying about what people will think.' She laid her hand lightly on his in genuine sympathy, knowing he would have a few very tough days ahead.

He grasped her arm. 'You're not going to throw yourself at Markland are you? I think even *you* might find yourself outclassed there.'

'My God,' she said, 'I'm glad Rick Markland came along if only to open my eyes and let me see you as the man you really are. I'm leaving now, Royston. I don't think we have anything more to say to one another.'

She walked out to the Jaguar, shattered and trembling and drove up to the spot Rick had taken her earlier on. She sat and watched the sun slide down to meet the dark line of hills. The sky was livid yellow, pregnant and uneasy with rain. She needed to walk, needed to think. She kicked off her shoes and let her bare feet feel the cool earth under the trees. Fat drops of rain began to fall, softly at first, then with increasing urgency until they formed a warm curtain of liquid. With her dress clinging to her skin, she ran back to the car and sat huddled in her seat, sodden with rain and misery, all washed up and stranded like an abandoned shipwreck.

* * *

'Darling! Where on earth have you been? It's past eleven! I've been out looking for you . . . '

Alexa drew back an arm, clenched a slender fist into a ball of iron and rammed it with violence into Rick's solar-plexus.

He gasped, but as she drew her arm back again, he intercepted the whirling, frenzied limb and held it rigid in the air before forcing it behind her back.

'You snake,' she breathed hoarsely, 'you lousy, rotten, crawling, double-dealing swine!'

He looked at her with momentary disbelief, then he started to grin. 'Any other labels to attach to me?' he asked amiably. 'A rat, a bastard? I think you've applied both of those previously.'

She struggled furiously to free her arm. She wanted to smash him to pieces.

'I rather think you've rumbled me,' he said softly.

'Yes!' she screamed in hurt and fury. 'Yes!'

'And I'd got it all planned to break the news gently.'

'Break it gently,' she exclaimed, 'would that make it all right? Aren't you ashamed of yourself? Is it just a big joke to you?' Hot tears gushed up behind her eyelids.

'Oh sweetheart,' he said gently, pulling her against him, 'of course it wasn't a joke. Look, come inside and let's talk about it.'

'*NO!*' She turned to leave.

He grasped her squirming, tormented body and enclosed it tightly in his arms. He carried her through into an airy sparsely furnished room lit softly by three spotlights shining onto the plain white walls, and laid her on a big old-fashioned sofa. She shivered in her damp clothes. The fight had all gone out of her. She was exhausted and the evening had ceased to have any firm reality.

Rick looked and behaved as he had always done — but could she believe in him any more? She could not bear to go on looking at him and transferred her attention to the room, noting the rows of books and tapes stacked against the wall, the wine rack full of dark inviting-looking bottles standing on a low shelf.

'You're soaking,' Rick murmured tenderly, unbuttoning her dress and slipping it down over her hips. He brought a thick cotton robe and wrapped it around her, placing a kiss on her neck.

'Will you have a glass of wine with me?' he asked with quiet concern.

She nodded, watching in a dreamlike state as he drew a cork from a dust-encrusted bottle. 'Château Latour 1973,' she murmured.

'Yes — my grandmother gave me it.' He handed her a fat goblet in which the liquid glinted like a dark jewel.

'*My* grandmother gives me tea and buttered scones!' she told him reproachfully.

His answering smile was rueful. 'My grandmother is rather rich. Do you mind?'

'I don't know,' she said wearily.

He took her hand, feeling it rest chilled and lifeless in his like a folded bat's wing. 'Oh my poor darling — you've had one hell of a day.'

She turned to face him, heavy-eyed and stunned. 'I told Royston. He didn't seem really upset,' she said slowly. 'I don't think he ever truly loved me. Isn't that terrible?'

Rick's blue eyes brimmed with tenderness. 'It would have been more terrible to have married him and found that out later.'

'Yes.' She sipped the wine. There were so many things she must say to Rick but they seemed muffled behind a thick curtain of velvet in her head. He made her feel secure; it always felt so *right* to be with him. She stared at him, at that strong, handsome yet infinitely sweet face that she had come to love so much. She trusted him. She really trusted him. Trust! Suddenly the word seemed tarnished. *She* had trusted, she had thrown caution to the winds. And what had Rick done? He had tricked her, betrayed her, used her. How could she ever forgive that? She had thought there was a little trifle to sort out about blonde leggy Penny; but the reality made that particular concern fade into trivial insignificance. She would have to tear him out of her heart, and the first step towards that goal was to demonstrate that she was strong enough to leave. Leave now!

'Don't look at me like that,' Rick

said, his voice low and pleading.

She searched around for her shoes.

'Hey! Where are you going?'

'I'm going home,' she said quietly, 'I'm going to go to bed and go to sleep — *on my own*. And in the morning I am going to get along with my work and my life with some semblance of efficiency and dignity.' She paused and then added with soft savagery, 'without the benefit of your presence, Rick.'

'Darling!' he protested moving towards her.

Anger exploded in her head. 'Don't call me darling. I'm not your darling, sweetheart, baby . . . any of those things. Can't you see how you've hurt me Rick? Hurt me where I'm most vulnerable. My work, my business means everything to me and you presumed to play around with all that just to give yourself a little amusement before you went back to bigger and better things in your tools empire. You weren't content with all your fun at Oxford, chasing girls and being a bit of a stud. That wasn't enough was it? A really rich, spoiled playboy can afford to indulge himself in something appropriately sophisticated — like taking a genuine, ordinary working woman for one hell of a ride. You must have had terrific fun. It must have made mere womanising look tame!'

'Stop it,' he said sharply, 'no one talks to me like that — not even you. What do you really know about me?'

'Not very much it seems.' Thoughts jostled in her head in dark, clashing colours; the deep reds and purples of rage. 'That's exactly it! What *do* I know about you, except that you're a joker who's no scruples about cheating and deceiving someone who was prepared in all good faith to give you a break!'

'Oh my God!' he groaned.

'It's time to grow up, Rick. Time to stop playing!'

'Hell! I've been working bloody hard!'

Just for a moment her mood softened. 'Yes, I'll give you that, but what about the rest; the sham of coming to me in need of a job? You must have thought I was the most gullible woman alive.'

'No,' he remonstrated calmly, 'I truly wanted to work for you. Right from the start. I was incredibly impressed.'

'Oh sure. But perhaps in time you were dying to give me one or two tips on how to improve things, how to develop my meagre skills!' Her fury had all surged up again.

'I think you run your business like a true pro. I'd do a deal with you any time; put money on you.'

'And you've plenty of that, haven't you. You were born with so many silver spoons in your mouth you must be rattling!'

'That's low and mean, Alexa; not worthy of you,' he said.

'Me, worthy! How can you? You're just like all the rest of the men, just as bad as Royston. Always ready to put a woman down!'

'That's rubbish,' he snapped. 'You're

all screwed up about being a woman; on the defensive all the time, thinking men are out to get the better of you.'

'Yes,' she yelled, 'I've learned the hard way — in business affairs and those of the heart.'

'Just calm down,' he said. 'You're as good as a man any day in my book — and rather better than most,' he added with a meaningful, seductive grin.

Her heart gave a wayward lurch. 'You're laughing at me,' she mourned, 'me and my struggling little firm.'

'Struggling! Now you're making me laugh.' His eyes twinkled merrily.

'Well small. Nothing like yours.' Her voice trailed off, beginning to lack conviction.

'Alexa, I found working for you full of challenge, immensely stimulating and intensely rewarding.'

'No,' she whispered, still tasting the sour view that Royston had fed her with. 'I don't know if I can believe that.' She silenced him as he tried to protest.

'But worst of all Rick, more wounding than anything was your continuing to deceive me — even when we, even when . . .'

'Even when we realised that we belong together body and soul?' he suggested helpfully.

'How could you do that?' she whispered in anguish. 'How could you?'

'Have you ever considered what it was like fighting your high principles regarding the pride of your dear Royston? Have you thought about the sheer mind-blowing desperation I felt; thinking that you would never bring yourself to hurt his self-esteem? Just imagine the insuperable advantage he would have gained by being the underdog. You'd have been so filled with compassion for him you'd have been marrying him by special licence the next day. You'd never ever have left him.'

She digested this new view of things with utter amazement. But it sounded so plausible; should she still be suspicious? Caution triumphed over sentiment. Once again she prepared to leave.

He stood in her way. 'Alexa, stop all this. Nothing has changed between us.'

'Everything has changed,' she said tragically.

'It's a matter of trust,' he said. 'That's all.'

She wanted to howl and scream in grief. She kept on walking.

She needed to find her dress.

'I still love you. I still want to marry you.' He turned her towards him and gazed at her for a long still moment. 'All right,' he said decisively, 'you think I'm just a rotten, double-dealing, woman-despising rat. I can see there's no point in trying to get any sense out of you tonight. So I'm not going to try any more. I'm a guy, O.K. That means I'm good for one or two things you won't get elsewhere.' He bent down and pulled her close.

'No, Rick. No!' she cried in panic.

'Yes,' he said, smiling with wicked

intimidation. 'Talking comes afterwards.'

He stood quite still. He made no attempt to force her. Alexa gazed up at him and then slowly, very slowly she placed herself close to him and slid her arms up around his neck.

'I've no choice but to trust you,' she murmured, 'anyone as doggedly persistent as you just must be the genuine article!'

'I'm your man,' he said, his eyes full of tender relief, 'that's all there is to it. Simple as that.'

'You beautiful, irresistible wretch,' she said. 'I shall love you for ever — damn you!'

'I should hope so.'

'And I want *everything*,' she sighed, her hand running over his neck and back.

His eyes were alive with merry wickedness. 'I had no intention of giving you anything less!'

He took her off to his bed and at last she felt the heaviness of his body lying over hers, delighted in the warmth of him inside her.

* * *

'Rick,' she said sheepishly much later, 'what about Penny with the long legs?'

He roared with laughter. 'You're going to be so disappointed. Penny has the flat upstairs. She's got a small baby and a husband away on a long trip with the Merchant Navy. She needs a little help sometimes and someone to talk to. O.K.?'

'O.K.'

'Now can we get back to more interesting pursuits?' he enquired.

He really was an impossibly energetic man.

* * *

On a day in late August, when the countryside flinched under the assault of the sun which beamed down in glistening gold ribbons, the iron gates guarding the entrance to Markland Hall swung aside to allow a big silver saloon car to pass through leaving a funnel of palest blue smoke laid on the gravel. The car gathered speed between the colonnade of trees, whose branches intertwined overhead in a gently swaying arch, then curved around in front of the house and coasted to a halt.

Alexa looked up at the graceful, faultless house, its big oak front door open in welcome behind the fat white flanking pillars. She had visited Rick's family home a number of times, yet still she felt a stab of alarm as the house came into view. An involuntary sigh escaped her.

Rick grinned. 'I used to have a few anxious moments wondering how to tell you about this little place!'

'I'll bet you did,' she chided. 'You certainly omitted to mention a few important facts about yourself when you came along asking for a job!'

'If I'd come to you as Richard

Markland of Markland Hall you wouldn't have taken my request very seriously would you?'

'No, I'm afraid not.'

He said softly. 'You just accepted me for what I was. That's when I started to love you.'

'Oh Rick — darling!' She traced a gentle loving path around his features with her fingers. 'Come on,' she whispered, 'Bess will think we've nothing better to do than make love all day.'

'What better thing is there to do?' he demanded.

Bess came to meet them in the hallway where the pungent smell of beeswax polish and freshly cut flowers reminded Rick powerfully of his childhood.

She had welcomed Alexa as a future granddaughter-in-law with a warmth that spoke of deep and genuine regard and already a bond had formed between the two women.

Alexa and Rick's wish to marry immediately and without fuss she had accepted readily. The only thing she insisted on was Rick's joining Markland's straight away. 'I'm past it,' she told him, 'and Markland's needs you.'

Hope, of course, had been totally delighted with the turn of events. 'Always knew you two were right for each other,' she told Alexa. 'And don't worry about Royston. He's been sighted,' she said, as though he were a piece of lost wreckage, 'in all the very best restaurants — with a stringy and exhausted blonde!'

Bess gave them lunch. Afterwards they sat sipping coffee and cognac.

Rick, relaxed and contented, leaned back in his chair and closed his eyes.

'You know,' Bess mused, 'I've been feeling a little useless and redundant since I retired from Markland's. I need fresh interest. I've been thinking of investing some money in a small growing business where I can be of some help, get involved, feel the excitement of starting again.'

Rick opened one eye. 'Go on,' he instructed.

'Lockton's would seem just the sort of expanding enterprise . . . '

'Have you two been scheming behind my back?' Rick wondered amiably.

'Mmn, strictly business,' Alexa murmured, smiling at him.

'You never breathed a word to me!'

Alexa arched her eyebrows, 'Well, sometimes it's best to keep one's little secrets — until the right time comes to reveal them!'

Rick did not fail to note the challenge. 'I think perhaps I deserved that. So — here's to the thriving of Lockton's and Markland's and enterprise in general!' He raised his glass.

'You just can't keep a good woman down!' Bess remarked with satisfaction.

'Quite,' Rick conceded, 'but there are still times when a man comes out on top!' He glanced at his wife with narrowed eyes.

She appeared disinclined to argue.

Their hands reached out and locked firmly together.

We do hope that you have enjoyed reading this large print book.

Did you know that all of our titles are available for purchase?

We publish a wide range of high quality large print books including:
Romances, Mysteries, Classics
General Fiction
Non Fiction and Westerns

Special interest titles available in large print are:
The Little Oxford Dictionary
Music Book, Song Book
Hymn Book, Service Book

Also available from us courtesy of Oxford University Press:
Young Readers' Dictionary
(large print edition)
Young Readers' Thesaurus
(large print edition)

For further information or a free brochure, please contact us at:

Other titles in the
Linford Romance Library:

CAVE OF FIRE

Rebecca King

Lost in a South American rain forest with sexy Nick Devlin, Dany knew she was a million miles away from the safe world represented by her fiancé, Marcus. Only goodness knew how she would be able to return to that world — for to return was one thing; to forget was another . . .

VOICES IN THE DARK

Mavis Thomas

Lucy Devereux survives a car accident, but loses her sight. She also discovers she has inherited her grandfather's fortune. Then, to her horror and amazement, a young man comes forward claiming to be her husband. Lucy has no memory of him at all, but Doctor Harvey Sheridan thinks this could be due to her head injuries. Powerless to resist, Lucy is taken to live with her professed husband's family and soon finds herself a virtual prisoner. Convinced they are conniving to get her money, she appeals for help to Doctor Sheridan . . .

TO FACE THE PAST

Karen Abbott

Eva Cunningham thought she had moved on since her devastating divorce from Matt Talbot three years ago, but when their paths cross again as newly appointed joint assistant managers of a struggling hotel in south Wales, she is forced to re-evaluate her feelings. However, Matt seems determined to date every female on the hotel staff — except her! And who is behind the perplexing incidents that threaten the hotel's future?

THE RECLUSE OF LONEWOOD PRIORY

Jasmina Svenne

When Isabel's father is attacked and injured, father and daughter are given shelter by Edmund Carwell, the owner of Longwood Priory. Intrigued by the fleeting glimpses of their mysterious benefactor, Isabel seeks him out, only to stumble on his tragic secret. She succeeds in bringing laughter and music back to the Priory. But is her influence strong enough to heal old wounds and help Carwell come to terms with the legacy of his past?